THE GRAPHIC NOVEL
William Shakespeare

ORIGINAL TEXT VERSION

Script Adaptation: John McDonald
Pencils: Neill Cameron
Inks: Bambos
Coloring: Jason Cardy & Kat Nicholson
Lettering: Nigel Dobbyn

American English Adaptation: Keith Howell
Design & Layout: Jo Wheeler & Greg Powell
Publishing Assistant: Joanna Watts
Additional Information: Karen Wenborn

Editor in Chief: Clive Bryant

Henry V: The Graphic Novel
Original Text Version

William Shakespeare

First US Edition

Published by: Classical Comics Ltd

Acknowledgments: Every effort has been made to trace copyright holders of
material reproduced in this book. Any rights not acknowledged here will be
acknowledged in subsequent editions if notice is given to Classical Comics Ltd.

All enquiries should be addressed to:
Classical Comics Ltd.
PO Box 7280
Litchborough
Towcester
NN12 9AR
United Kingdom

Email: info@classicalcomics.com
Web: www.classicalcomics.com

ISBN: 978-1-906332-41-9

Printed by SURE Print & Design
using biodegradable vegetable inks on environmentally friendly paper.
This material can be disposed of by recycling,
incineration for energy recovery, composting and biodegradation.

Contents

Dramatis Personæ

King Henry the Fifth
King of England

Duke Of Gloucester
Brother to the King

Duke Of Bedford
Brother to the King

Duke Of Exeter
Uncle to the King

Duke Of York
Cousin to the King

Earl Of Salisbury

Earl Of Westmoreland

Earl Of Warwick

Archbishop Of Canterbury

Bishop Of Ely

Earl Of Cambridge
Conspirator

Henry, Lord Scroop of Masham
Conspirator

Sir Thomas Grey
Conspirator

Sir Thomas Erpingham
Officer in King Henry's army

Captain Gower
Officer in King Henry's army

Captain Fluellen
Officer in King Henry's army

Captain Macmorris
Officer in King Henry's army

Captain Jamy
Officer in King Henry's army

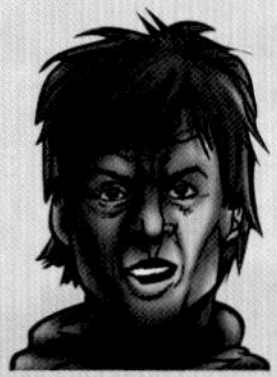

John Bates
Soldier in King Henry's army

Alexander Court
Soldier in King Henry's army

4

Dramatis Personæ

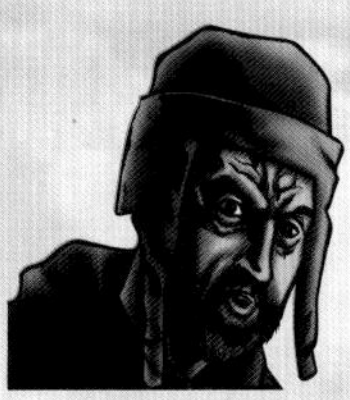

Michael Williams
Soldier in
King Henry's army

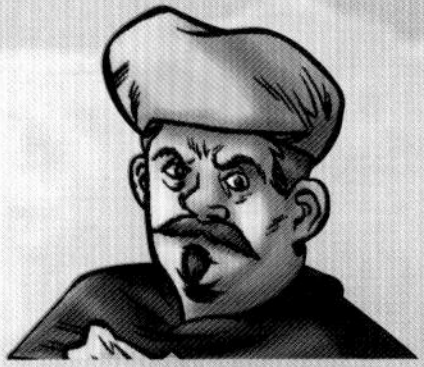

Pistol
Soldier in
King Henry's army

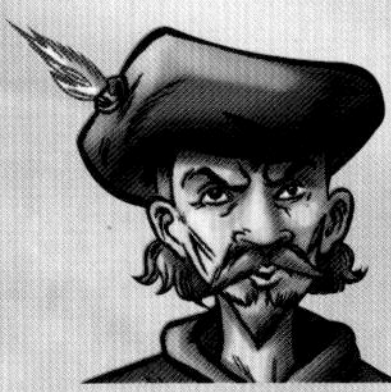

Nym
Soldier in
King Henry's army

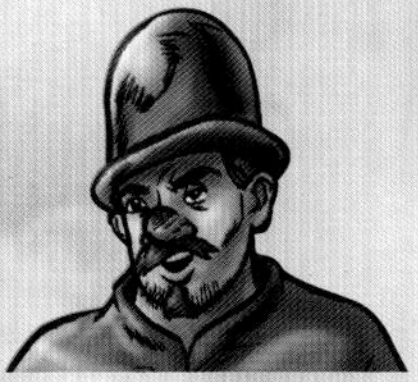

Bardolph
Soldier in
King Henry's army

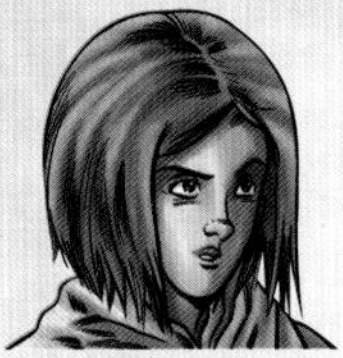

Boy
Servant

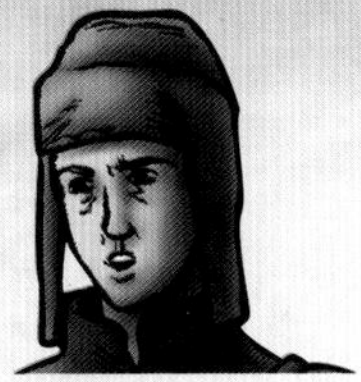

A Herald

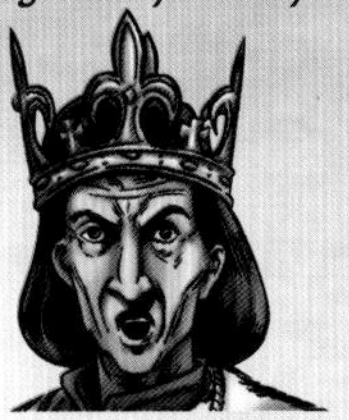

Charles the Sixth
King of France

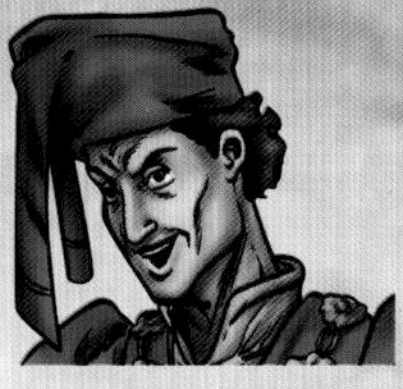

Lewis
The Dauphin

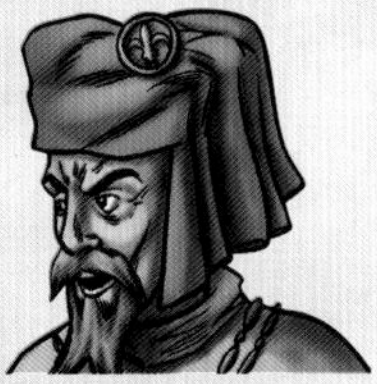

Duke Of Bourbon
French Duke

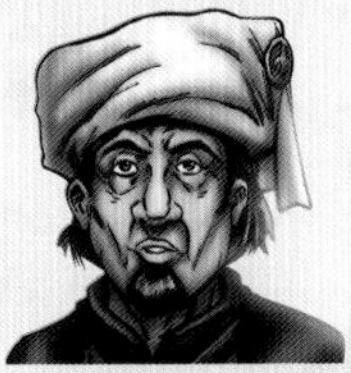

Duke Of Burgundy
French Duke

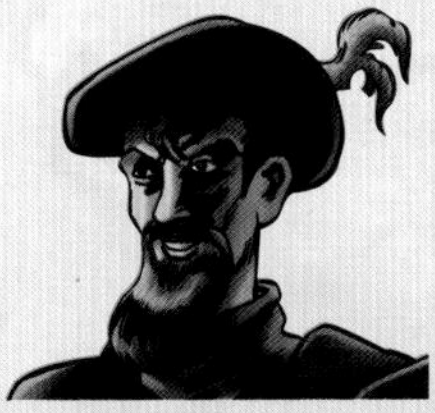

Duke Of Orleans
French Duke

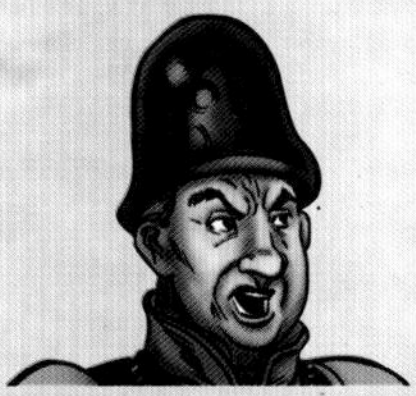

The Constable of France

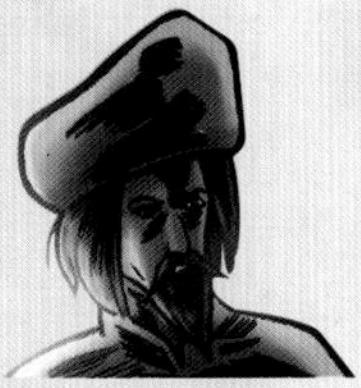

Lord Rambures
French Lord

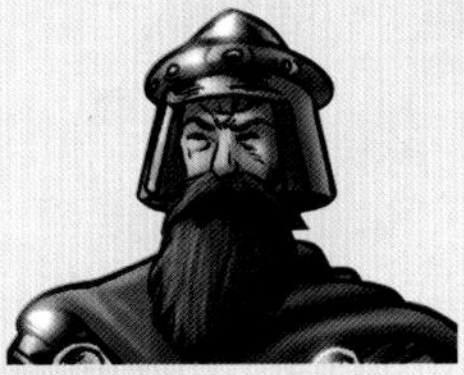

Lord Grandpré
French Lord

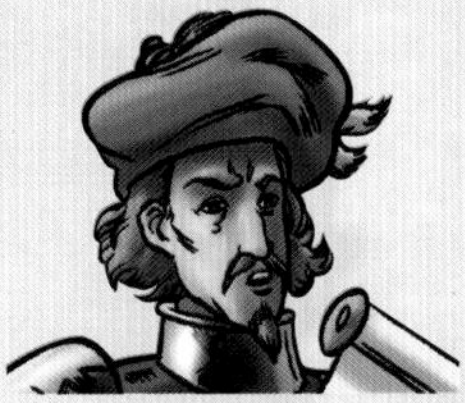

Montjoy
French Herald

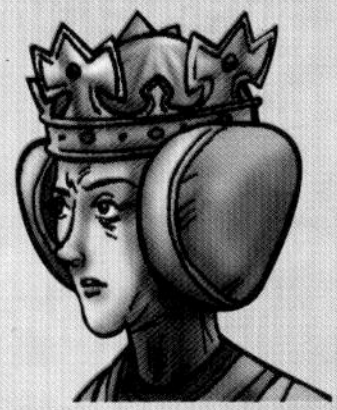

Queen Isabel
Queen of France

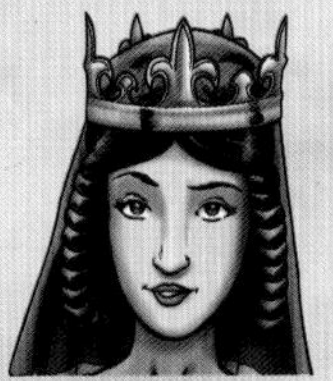

Katherine
Daughter to
Charles and Isabel

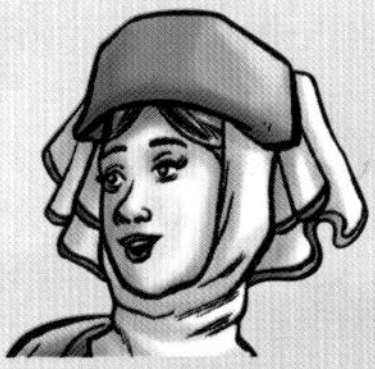

Alice
A lady attending on
Katherine

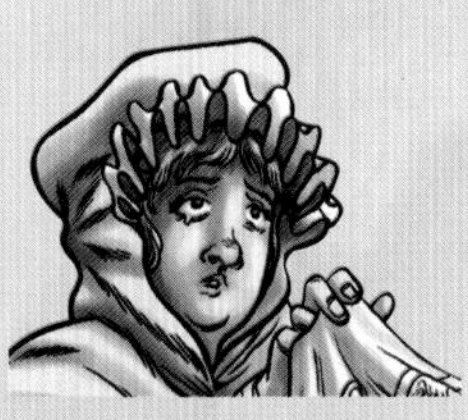

Hostess of a tavern
Formerly Mistress
Quickly

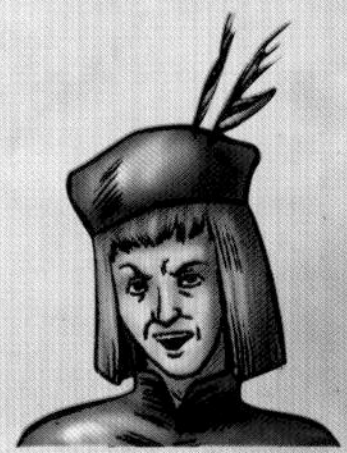

Chorus

A Note on Pronunciation

As you go through this Original Text version, you will notice how some words that usually end in "-ed" are written "-'d" whereas others are written out in full.

Shakespeare wrote much of his plays in verse, where the rhythm of the speech formed strings of "iambic pentameters", each line being five pairs of syllables, with the second syllable in each pair being the most dominant in the rhythm.

To help with enunciation and voice projection in early theaters, words that ended with "-ed" had that last syllable accented – unless to do so would have spoiled the iambic rhythm, in which case it was spoken just as we say the word today.

This speech by Macbeth:

"Accursed be that tongue that tells me so,"

would have been said as:

"Accurse–ed be that tongue that tells me so,"

so that the syllable pairs (five of them in the line) are correct in number and in emphasis (if you say it as "accurs'd" you'll see how the rhythm of the line is destroyed).

Whereas:

"And damn'd be him that first cries, 'Hold enough!' "

cannot be pronounced "dam-ned" because to do so would give eleven syllables in the line, and would not allow the right emphasis to be placed on each syllable.

In short, whenever you see a word ending "-ed" it should have its "e" pronounced to preserve the rhythm of the speech.

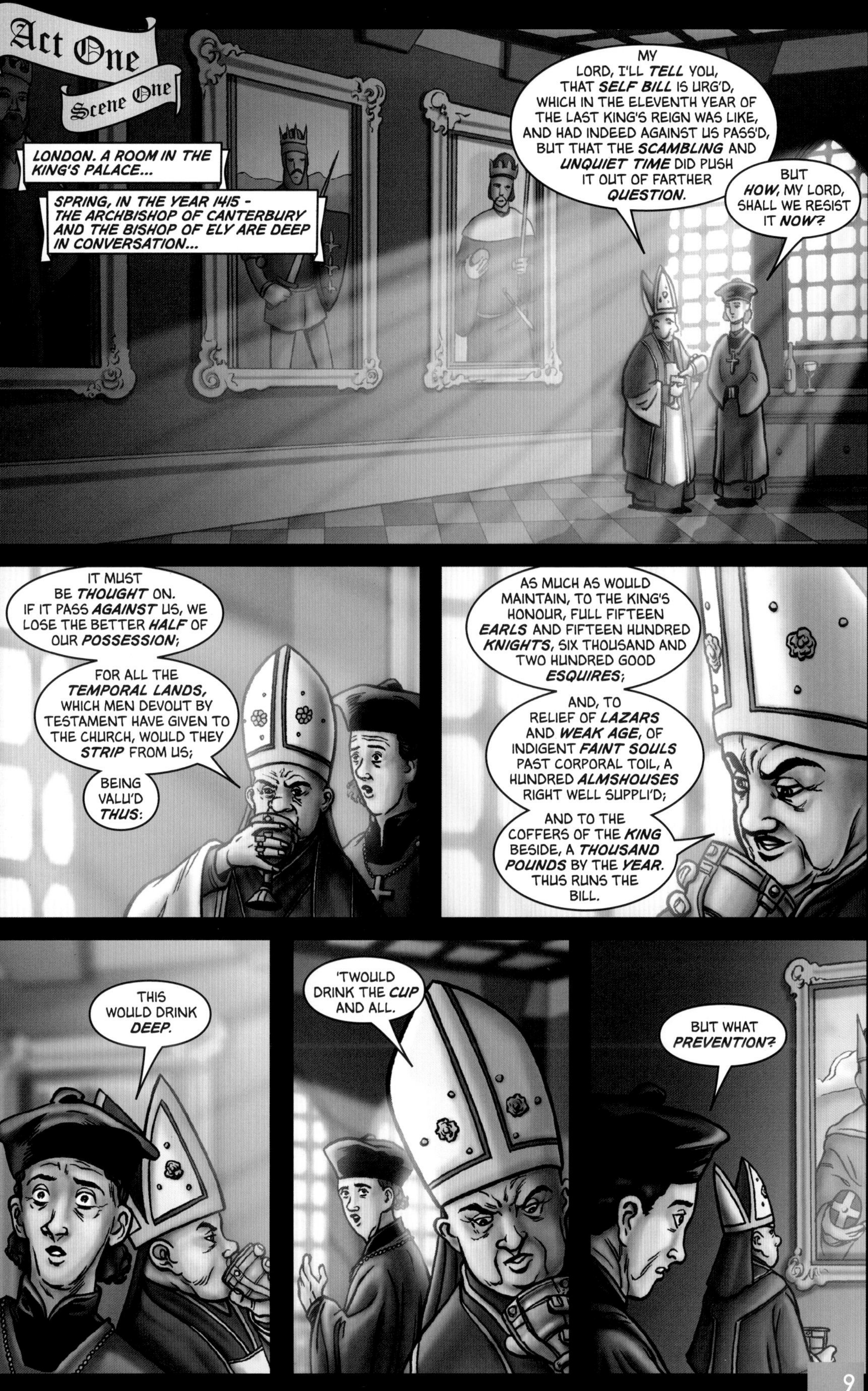
Act One
Scene One
LONDON. A ROOM IN THE KING'S PALACE...
SPRING, IN THE YEAR 1415 - THE ARCHBISHOP OF CANTERBURY AND THE BISHOP OF ELY ARE DEEP IN CONVERSATION...
MY LORD, I'LL TELL YOU, THAT SELF BILL IS URG'D, WHICH IN THE ELEVENTH YEAR OF THE LAST KING'S REIGN WAS LIKE, AND HAD INDEED AGAINST US PASS'D, BUT THAT THE SCAMBLING AND UNQUIET TIME DID PUSH IT OUT OF FARTHER QUESTION.
BUT HOW, MY LORD, SHALL WE RESIST IT NOW?
IT MUST BE THOUGHT ON. IF IT PASS AGAINST US, WE LOSE THE BETTER HALF OF OUR POSSESSION;
FOR ALL THE TEMPORAL LANDS, WHICH MEN DEVOUT BY TESTAMENT HAVE GIVEN TO THE CHURCH, WOULD THEY STRIP FROM US;
BEING VALU'D THUS:
AS MUCH AS WOULD MAINTAIN, TO THE KING'S HONOUR, FULL FIFTEEN EARLS AND FIFTEEN HUNDRED KNIGHTS, SIX THOUSAND AND TWO HUNDRED GOOD ESQUIRES;
AND, TO RELIEF OF LAZARS AND WEAK AGE, OF INDIGENT FAINT SOULS PAST CORPORAL TOIL, A HUNDRED ALMSHOUSES RIGHT WELL SUPPLI'D;
AND TO THE COFFERS OF THE KING BESIDE, A THOUSAND POUNDS BY THE YEAR. THUS RUNS THE BILL.
THIS WOULD DRINK DEEP.
'TWOULD DRINK THE CUP AND ALL.
BUT WHAT PREVENTION?

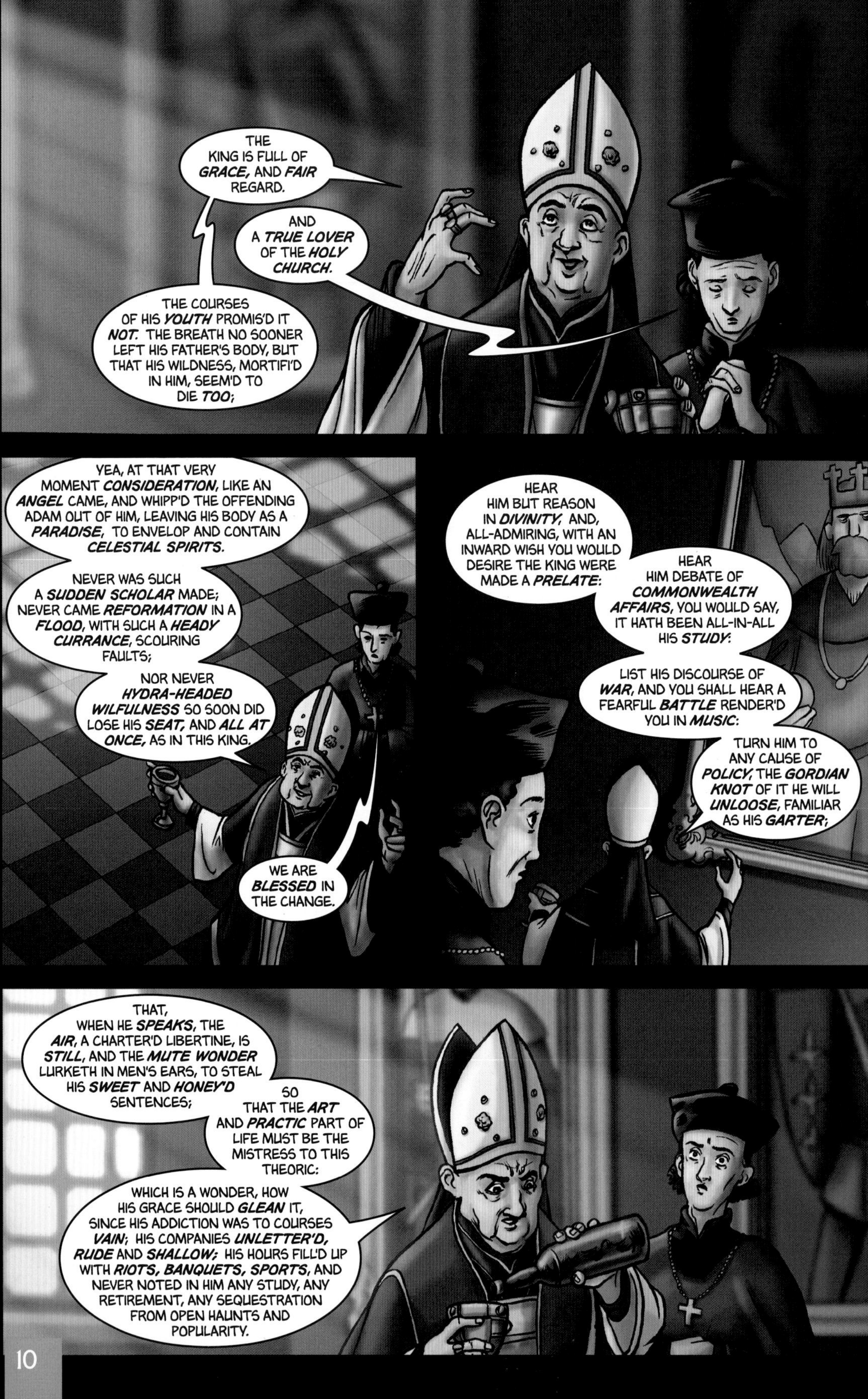
THE KING IS FULL OF GRACE, AND FAIR REGARD.
AND A TRUE LOVER OF THE HOLY CHURCH.
THE COURSES OF HIS YOUTH PROMIS'D IT NOT. THE BREATH NO SOONER LEFT HIS FATHER'S BODY, BUT THAT HIS WILDNESS, MORTIFI'D IN HIM, SEEM'D TO DIE TOO;
YEA, AT THAT VERY MOMENT CONSIDERATION, LIKE AN ANGEL CAME, AND WHIPP'D THE OFFENDING ADAM OUT OF HIM, LEAVING HIS BODY AS A PARADISE, TO ENVELOP AND CONTAIN CELESTIAL SPIRITS.
NEVER WAS SUCH A SUDDEN SCHOLAR MADE; NEVER CAME REFORMATION IN A FLOOD, WITH SUCH A HEADY CURRANCE, SCOURING FAULTS;
NOR NEVER HYDRA-HEADED WILFULNESS SO SOON DID LOSE HIS SEAT, AND ALL AT ONCE, AS IN THIS KING.
WE ARE BLESSED IN THE CHANGE.
HEAR HIM BUT REASON IN DIVINITY, AND, ALL-ADMIRING, WITH AN INWARD WISH YOU WOULD DESIRE THE KING WERE MADE A PRELATE:
HEAR HIM DEBATE OF COMMONWEALTH AFFAIRS, YOU WOULD SAY, IT HATH BEEN ALL-IN-ALL HIS STUDY:
LIST HIS DISCOURSE OF WAR, AND YOU SHALL HEAR A FEARFUL BATTLE RENDER'D YOU IN MUSIC:
TURN HIM TO ANY CAUSE OF POLICY, THE GORDIAN KNOT OF IT HE WILL UNLOOSE, FAMILIAR AS HIS GARTER;
THAT, WHEN HE SPEAKS, THE AIR, A CHARTER'D LIBERTINE, IS STILL, AND THE MUTE WONDER LURKETH IN MEN'S EARS, TO STEAL HIS SWEET AND HONEY'D SENTENCES;
SO THAT THE ART AND PRACTIC PART OF LIFE MUST BE THE MISTRESS TO THIS THEORIC:
WHICH IS A WONDER, HOW HIS GRACE SHOULD GLEAN IT, SINCE HIS ADDICTION WAS TO COURSES VAIN; HIS COMPANIES UNLETTER'D, RUDE AND SHALLOW; HIS HOURS FILL'D UP WITH RIOTS, BANQUETS, SPORTS, AND NEVER NOTED IN HIM ANY STUDY, ANY RETIREMENT, ANY SEQUESTRATION FROM OPEN HAUNTS AND POPULARITY.

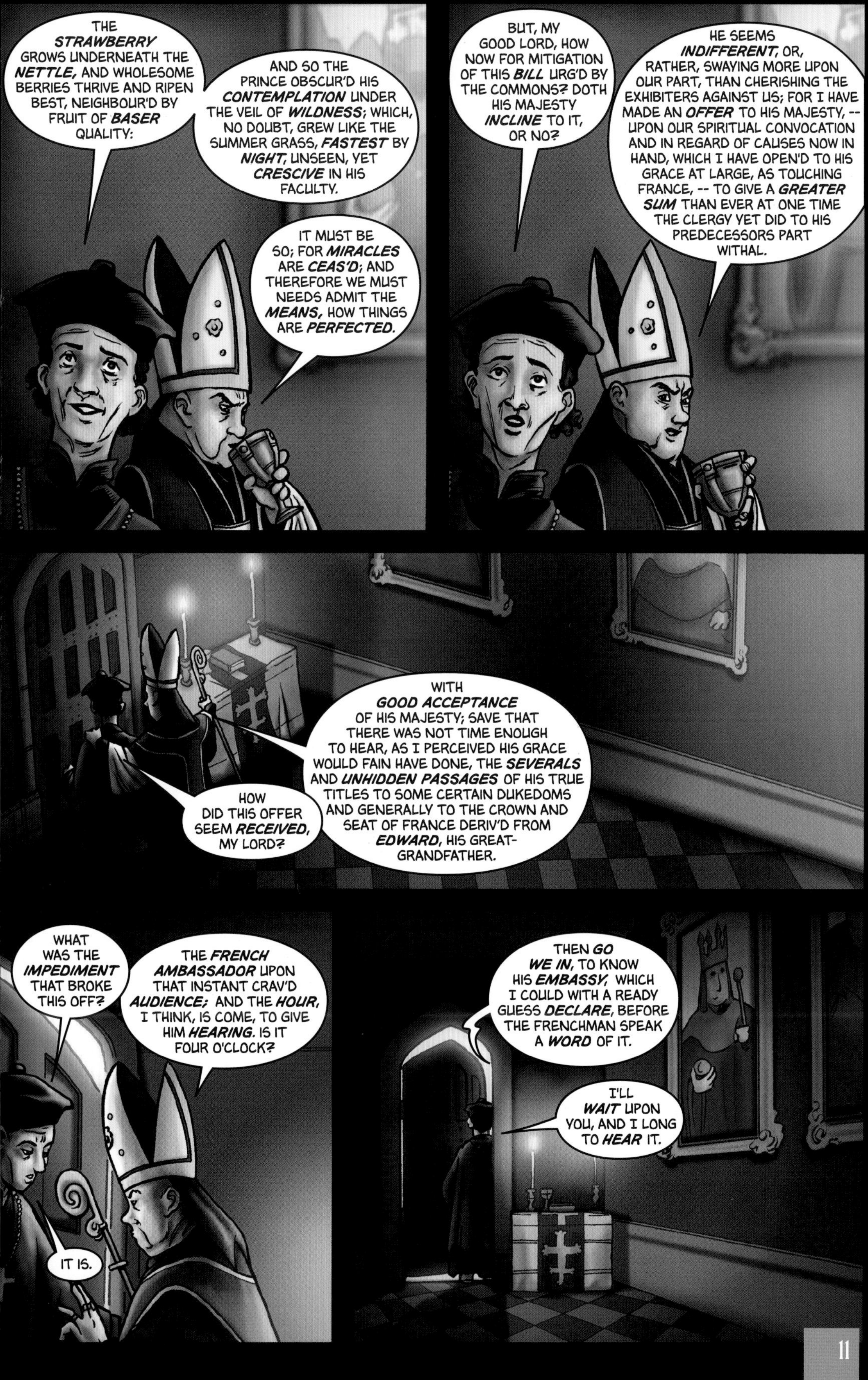
THE STRAWBERRY GROWS UNDERNEATH THE NETTLE, AND WHOLESOME BERRIES THRIVE AND RIPEN BEST, NEIGHBOUR'D BY FRUIT OF BASER QUALITY:
AND SO THE PRINCE OBSCUR'D HIS CONTEMPLATION UNDER THE VEIL OF WILDNESS; WHICH, NO DOUBT, GREW LIKE THE SUMMER GRASS, FASTEST BY NIGHT, UNSEEN, YET CRESCIVE IN HIS FACULTY.
IT MUST BE SO; FOR MIRACLES ARE CEAS'D; AND THEREFORE WE MUST NEEDS ADMIT THE MEANS, HOW THINGS ARE PERFECTED.
BUT, MY GOOD LORD, HOW NOW FOR MITIGATION OF THIS BILL URG'D BY THE COMMONS? DOTH HIS MAJESTY INCLINE TO IT, OR NO?
HE SEEMS INDIFFERENT, OR, RATHER, SWAYING MORE UPON OUR PART, THAN CHERISHING THE EXHIBITERS AGAINST US; FOR I HAVE MADE AN OFFER TO HIS MAJESTY, -- UPON OUR SPIRITUAL CONVOCATION AND IN REGARD OF CAUSES NOW IN HAND, WHICH I HAVE OPEN'D TO HIS GRACE AT LARGE, AS TOUCHING FRANCE, -- TO GIVE A GREATER SUM THAN EVER AT ONE TIME THE CLERGY YET DID TO HIS PREDECESSORS PART WITHAL.
HOW DID THIS OFFER SEEM RECEIVED, MY LORD?
WITH GOOD ACCEPTANCE OF HIS MAJESTY; SAVE THAT THERE WAS NOT TIME ENOUGH TO HEAR, AS I PERCEIVED HIS GRACE WOULD FAIN HAVE DONE, THE SEVERALS AND UNHIDDEN PASSAGES OF HIS TRUE TITLES TO SOME CERTAIN DUKEDOMS AND GENERALLY TO THE CROWN AND SEAT OF FRANCE DERIV'D FROM EDWARD, HIS GREAT-GRANDFATHER.
WHAT WAS THE IMPEDIMENT THAT BROKE THIS OFF?
THE FRENCH AMBASSADOR UPON THAT INSTANT CRAV'D AUDIENCE; AND THE HOUR, I THINK, IS COME, TO GIVE HIM HEARING. IS IT FOUR O'CLOCK?
IT IS.
THEN GO WE IN, TO KNOW HIS EMBASSY, WHICH I COULD WITH A READY GUESS DECLARE, BEFORE THE FRENCHMAN SPEAK A WORD OF IT.
I'LL WAIT UPON YOU, AND I LONG TO HEAR IT.

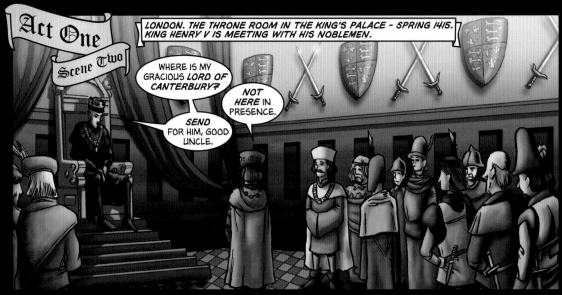

LONDON. THE THRONE ROOM IN THE KING'S PALACE - SPRING 1415. KING HENRY V IS MEETING WITH HIS NOBLEMEN.

WHERE IS MY GRACIOUS *LORD OF CANTERBURY?*

NOT HERE IN PRESENCE.

SEND FOR HIM, GOOD UNCLE.

SHALL WE CALL IN THE *AMBASSADOR,* MY LIEGE?

NOT YET, MY COUSIN: WE WOULD BE RESOLV'D, BEFORE WE HEAR HIM, OF SOME THINGS OF WEIGHT THAT TASK OUR THOUGHTS, CONCERNING US AND *FRANCE.*

GOD AND HIS *ANGELS* GUARD YOUR SACRED THRONE AND MAKE YOU *LONG* BECOME IT!

SURE, WE *THANK* YOU.

MY LEARNED LORD, WE PRAY YOU TO PROCEED, AND *JUSTLY* AND *RELIGIOUSLY* UNFOLD, WHY THE *LAW SALIQUE* THAT THEY HAVE IN FRANCE, OR SHOULD, OR SHOULD NOT, *BAR* US IN OUR *CLAIM.*

AND GOD *FORBID,* MY DEAR AND FAITHFUL LORD, THAT YOU SHOULD *FASHION, WREST,* OR *BOW* YOUR READING, OR NICELY CHARGE YOUR UNDERSTANDING SOUL. WITH OPENING TITLES MISCREATE, WHOSE RIGHT SUITS NOT IN NATIVE COLOURS WITH THE *TRUTH;*

FOR *GOD* DOTH KNOW, HOW MANY, NOW IN HEALTH, SHALL DROP THEIR *BLOOD* IN APPROBATION OF WHAT YOUR REVERENCE SHALL INCITE US TO. THEREFORE TAKE HEED HOW YOU *IMPAWN* OUR PERSON, HOW YOU AWAKE OUR SLEEPING *SWORD OF WAR:*

WE *CHARGE* YOU, IN THE NAME OF *GOD,* TAKE *HEED;*

FOR NEVER TWO SUCH KINGDOMS DID CONTEND WITHOUT MUCH FALL OF *BLOOD;* WHOSE *GUILTLESS DROPS* ARE EVERY ONE A *WOE,* A *SORE COMPLAINT* 'GAINST HIM WHOSE WRONGS GIVE EDGE UNTO THE SWORDS THAT MAKE SUCH WASTE IN BRIEF MORTALITY.

UNDER THIS CONJURATION, *SPEAK,* MY LORD, AND WE WILL HEAR, NOTE, AND BELIEVE IN HEART, THAT WHAT YOU SPEAK IS IN YOUR *CONSCIENCE* WASH'D, AS PURE AS *SIN* WITH *BAPTISM.*

O, LET THEIR BODIES FOLLOW, MY DEAR LIEGE, WITH *BLOOD,* AND *SWORD,* AND *FIRE;* TO WIN YOUR RIGHT: IN AID WHEREOF, WE OF THE *SPIRITUALTY* WILL RAISE YOUR HIGHNESS SUCH A MIGHTY SUM, AS NEVER DID THE CLERGY AT ONE TIME BRING IN TO ANY OF YOUR ANCESTORS.

WE MUST NOT ONLY ARM TO INVADE THE *FRENCH,* BUT LAY DOWN OUR PROPORTIONS TO DEFEND AGAINST THE *SCOT,* WHO WILL MAKE *ROAD* UPON US WITH ALL ADVANTAGES.

THEY OF THOSE *MARCHES,* GRACIOUS SOVEREIGN, SHALL BE A WALL SUFFICIENT TO DEFEND OUR INLAND FROM THE PILFERING *BORDERERS.*

WE DO NOT MEAN THE *COURSING SNATCHERS* ONLY, BUT FEAR THE *MAIN INTENDMENT* OF THE SCOT, WHO HATH BEEN STILL A GIDDY NEIGHBOUR TO US; FOR YOU SHALL READ, THAT MY *GREAT-GRANDFATHER* NEVER WENT WITH HIS FORCES INTO FRANCE, BUT THAT THE *SCOT* ON HIS *UNFURNISH'D KINGDOM* CAME *POURING,* LIKE THE *TIDE* INTO A *BREACH,* WITH AMPLE AND BRIM FULLNESS OF HIS FORCE, GALLING THE GLEANED LAND WITH HOT ASSAYS, GIRDING WITH GRIEVOUS SIEGE CASTLES AND TOWNS;

THAT *ENGLAND,* BEING *EMPTY* OF DEFENCE, HATH *SHOOK* AND *TREMBLED* AT THE ILL NEIGHBOUR-HOOD.

SHE HATH BEEN THEN MORE *FEAR'D* THAN *HARM'D,* MY LIEGE;

FOR HEAR HER BUT EXAMPL'D BY HERSELF: WHEN ALL HER CHIVALRY HATH BEEN IN *FRANCE,* AND SHE A MOURNING WIDOW OF HER NOBLES, SHE HATH HERSELF NOT ONLY *WELL DEFENDED,* BUT TAKEN, AND IMPOUNDED AS A *STRAY,* THE KING OF SCOTS; WHOM SHE DID SEND TO *FRANCE,* TO FILL KING EDWARD'S FAME WITH *PRISONER KINGS,* AND MAKE HER CHRONICLE AS *RICH* WITH *PRAISE,* AS IS THE OOZE AND BOTTOM OF THE SEA WITH *SUNKEN WRECK* AND *SUMLESS TREASURIES.*

BUT THERE'S A SAYING, VERY OLD AND TRUE, "IF THAT YOU WILL *FRANCE* WIN, THEN WITH *SCOTLAND* FIRST BEGIN:"

FOR ONCE THE EAGLE ENGLAND BEING IN PREY, TO HER UNGUARDED NEST THE WEASEL *SCOT* COMES SNEAKING AND SO SUCKS HER PRINCELY EGGS; PLAYING THE *MOUSE* IN ABSENCE OF THE *CAT;* TO TEAR AND HAVOC MORE THAN SHE CAN *EAT.*

IT FOLLOWS THEN, THE *CAT* MUST STAY AT *HOME:* YET THAT IS BUT A CRUSH'D NECESSITY; SINCE WE HAVE *LOCKS* TO SAFEGUARD NECESSARIES, AND *PRETTY TRAPS* TO CATCH THE *PETTY THIEVES.*

WHILE THAT THE ARMED HAND DOTH FIGHT ABROAD, THE ADVISED HEAD DEFENDS ITSELF AT *HOME:* FOR GOVERNMENT, THOUGH HIGH, AND LOW, AND LOWER, PUT INTO PARTS, DOTH KEEP IN ONE CONSENT, CONGREEING IN A FULL AND NATURAL CLOSE, LIKE *MUSIC.*

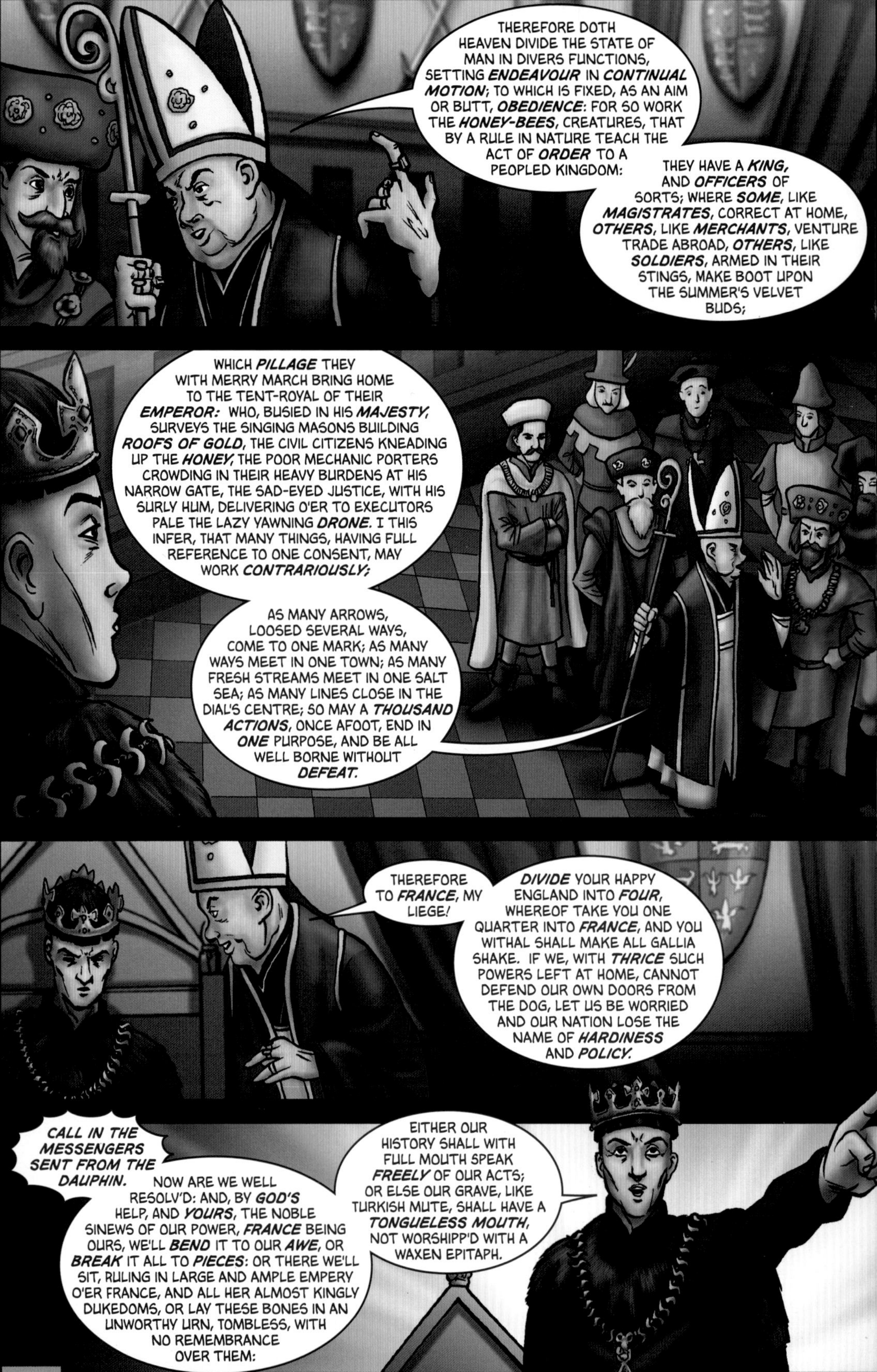
THEREFORE DOTH HEAVEN DIVIDE THE STATE OF MAN IN DIVERS FUNCTIONS, SETTING ENDEAVOUR IN CONTINUAL MOTION; TO WHICH IS FIXED, AS AN AIM OR BUTT, OBEDIENCE: FOR SO WORK THE HONEY-BEES, CREATURES, THAT BY A RULE IN NATURE TEACH THE ACT OF ORDER TO A PEOPLED KINGDOM:
THEY HAVE A KING, AND OFFICERS OF SORTS; WHERE SOME, LIKE MAGISTRATES, CORRECT AT HOME, OTHERS, LIKE MERCHANTS, VENTURE TRADE ABROAD, OTHERS, LIKE SOLDIERS, ARMED IN THEIR STINGS, MAKE BOOT UPON THE SUMMER'S VELVET BUDS;
WHICH PILLAGE THEY WITH MERRY MARCH BRING HOME TO THE TENT-ROYAL OF THEIR EMPEROR: WHO, BUSIED IN HIS MAJESTY, SURVEYS THE SINGING MASONS BUILDING ROOFS OF GOLD, THE CIVIL CITIZENS KNEADING UP THE HONEY, THE POOR MECHANIC PORTERS CROWDING IN THEIR HEAVY BURDENS AT HIS NARROW GATE, THE SAD-EYED JUSTICE, WITH HIS SURLY HUM, DELIVERING O'ER TO EXECUTORS PALE THE LAZY YAWNING DRONE. I THIS INFER, THAT MANY THINGS, HAVING FULL REFERENCE TO ONE CONSENT, MAY WORK CONTRARIOUSLY;
AS MANY ARROWS, LOOSED SEVERAL WAYS, COME TO ONE MARK; AS MANY WAYS MEET IN ONE TOWN; AS MANY FRESH STREAMS MEET IN ONE SALT SEA; AS MANY LINES CLOSE IN THE DIAL'S CENTRE; SO MAY A THOUSAND ACTIONS, ONCE AFOOT, END IN ONE PURPOSE, AND BE ALL WELL BORNE WITHOUT DEFEAT.
THEREFORE TO FRANCE, MY LIEGE!
DIVIDE YOUR HAPPY ENGLAND INTO FOUR, WHEREOF TAKE YOU ONE QUARTER INTO FRANCE, AND YOU WITHAL SHALL MAKE ALL GALLIA SHAKE. IF WE, WITH THRICE SUCH POWERS LEFT AT HOME, CANNOT DEFEND OUR OWN DOORS FROM THE DOG, LET US BE WORRIED AND OUR NATION LOSE THE NAME OF HARDINESS AND POLICY.
CALL IN THE MESSENGERS SENT FROM THE DAUPHIN.
NOW ARE WE WELL RESOLV'D: AND, BY GOD'S HELP, AND YOURS, THE NOBLE SINEWS OF OUR POWER, FRANCE BEING OURS, WE'LL BEND IT TO OUR AWE, OR BREAK IT ALL TO PIECES: OR THERE WE'LL SIT, RULING IN LARGE AND AMPLE EMPERY O'ER FRANCE, AND ALL HER ALMOST KINGLY DUKEDOMS, OR LAY THESE BONES IN AN UNWORTHY URN, TOMBLESS, WITH NO REMEMBRANCE OVER THEM:
EITHER OUR HISTORY SHALL WITH FULL MOUTH SPEAK FREELY OF OUR ACTS; OR ELSE OUR GRAVE, LIKE TURKISH MUTE, SHALL HAVE A TONGUELESS MOUTH, NOT WORSHIPP'D WITH A WAXEN EPITAPH.

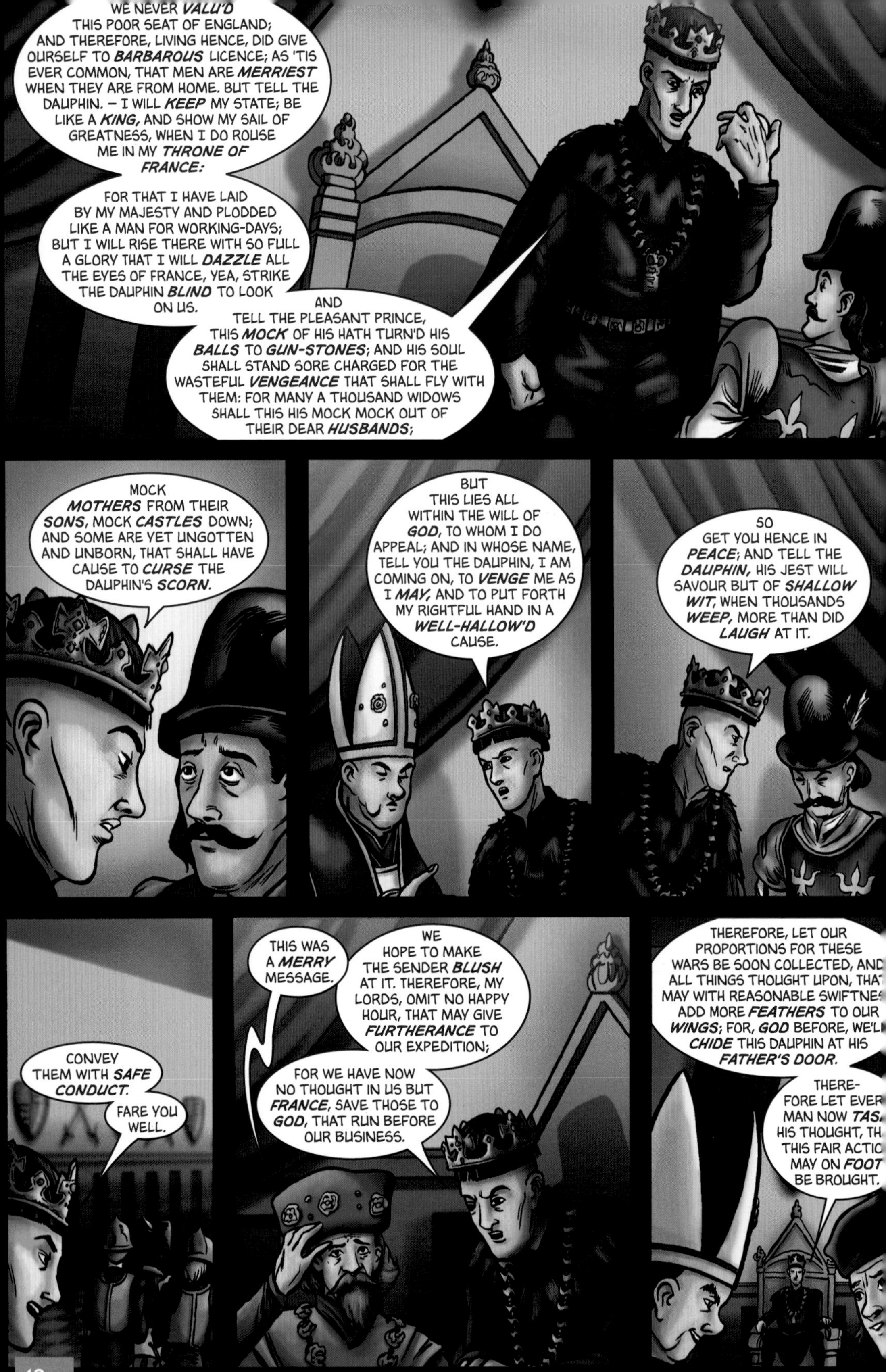
WE NEVER VALU'D THIS POOR SEAT OF ENGLAND; AND THEREFORE, LIVING HENCE, DID GIVE OURSELF TO BARBAROUS LICENCE; AS 'TIS EVER COMMON, THAT MEN ARE MERRIEST WHEN THEY ARE FROM HOME. BUT TELL THE DAUPHIN. – I WILL KEEP MY STATE; BE LIKE A KING, AND SHOW MY SAIL OF GREATNESS, WHEN I DO ROUSE ME IN MY THRONE OF FRANCE:
FOR THAT I HAVE LAID BY MY MAJESTY AND PLODDED LIKE A MAN FOR WORKING-DAYS; BUT I WILL RISE THERE WITH SO FULL A GLORY THAT I WILL DAZZLE ALL THE EYES OF FRANCE, YEA, STRIKE THE DAUPHIN BLIND TO LOOK ON US.
AND TELL THE PLEASANT PRINCE, THIS MOCK OF HIS HATH TURN'D HIS BALLS TO GUN-STONES; AND HIS SOUL SHALL STAND SORE CHARGED FOR THE WASTEFUL VENGEANCE THAT SHALL FLY WITH THEM: FOR MANY A THOUSAND WIDOWS SHALL THIS HIS MOCK MOCK OUT OF THEIR DEAR HUSBANDS;
MOCK MOTHERS FROM THEIR SONS, MOCK CASTLES DOWN; AND SOME ARE YET UNGOTTEN AND UNBORN, THAT SHALL HAVE CAUSE TO CURSE THE DAUPHIN'S SCORN.
BUT THIS LIES ALL WITHIN THE WILL OF GOD, TO WHOM I DO APPEAL; AND IN WHOSE NAME, TELL YOU THE DAUPHIN, I AM COMING ON, TO VENGE ME AS I MAY, AND TO PUT FORTH MY RIGHTFUL HAND IN A WELL-HALLOW'D CAUSE.
SO GET YOU HENCE IN PEACE; AND TELL THE DAUPHIN, HIS JEST WILL SAVOUR BUT OF SHALLOW WIT, WHEN THOUSANDS WEEP, MORE THAN DID LAUGH AT IT.
CONVEY THEM WITH SAFE CONDUCT.
FARE YOU WELL.
THIS WAS A MERRY MESSAGE.
WE HOPE TO MAKE THE SENDER BLUSH AT IT. THEREFORE, MY LORDS, OMIT NO HAPPY HOUR, THAT MAY GIVE FURTHERANCE TO OUR EXPEDITION;
FOR WE HAVE NOW NO THOUGHT IN US BUT FRANCE, SAVE THOSE TO GOD, THAT RUN BEFORE OUR BUSINESS.
THEREFORE, LET OUR PROPORTIONS FOR THESE WARS BE SOON COLLECTED, AND ALL THINGS THOUGHT UPON, THAT MAY WITH REASONABLE SWIFTNES ADD MORE FEATHERS TO OUR WINGS; FOR, GOD BEFORE, WE'L CHIDE THIS DAUPHIN AT HIS FATHER'S DOOR.
THERE-FORE LET EVER MAN NOW TAS HIS THOUGHT, TH THIS FAIR ACTIO MAY ON FOOT BE BROUGHT.

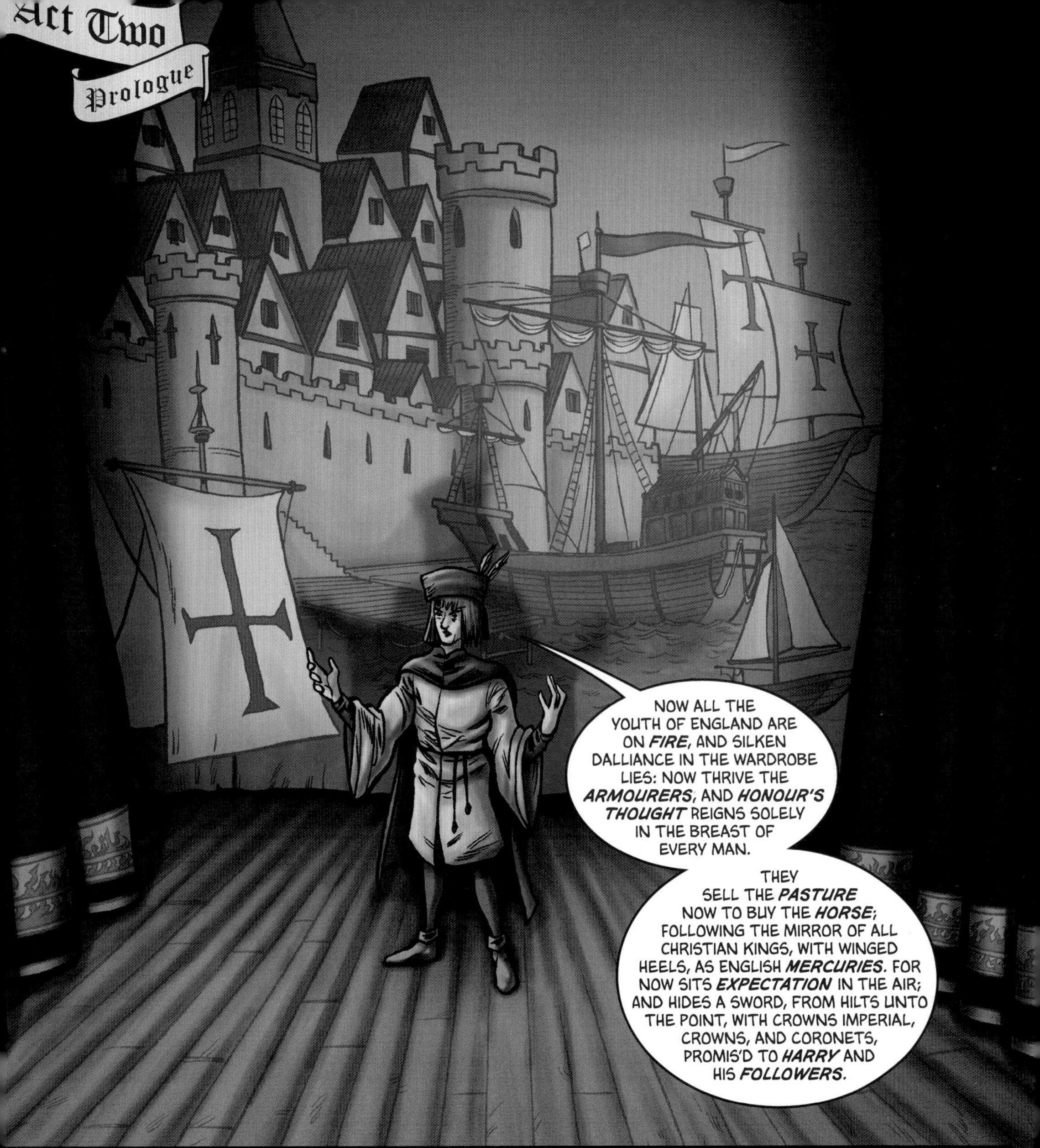
Act Two
Prologue
NOW ALL THE YOUTH OF ENGLAND ARE ON FIRE, AND SILKEN DALLIANCE IN THE WARDROBE LIES: NOW THRIVE THE ARMOURERS, AND HONOUR'S THOUGHT REIGNS SOLELY IN THE BREAST OF EVERY MAN.
THEY SELL THE PASTURE NOW TO BUY THE HORSE; FOLLOWING THE MIRROR OF ALL CHRISTIAN KINGS, WITH WINGED HEELS, AS ENGLISH MERCURIES. FOR NOW SITS EXPECTATION IN THE AIR; AND HIDES A SWORD, FROM HILTS UNTO THE POINT, WITH CROWNS IMPERIAL, CROWNS, AND CORONETS, PROMIS'D TO HARRY AND HIS FOLLOWERS.

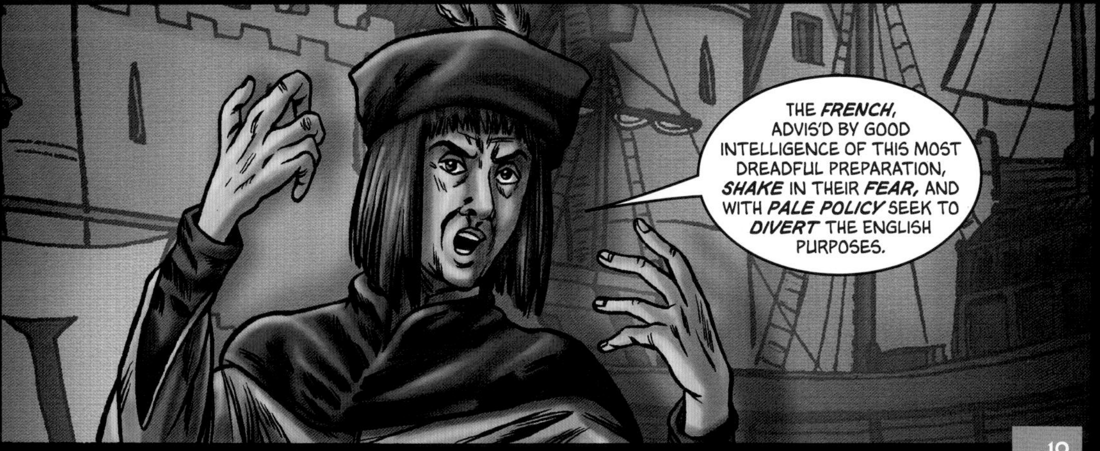
THE FRENCH, ADVIS'D BY GOOD INTELLIGENCE OF THIS MOST DREADFUL PREPARATION, SHAKE IN THEIR FEAR, AND WITH PALE POLICY SEEK TO DIVERT THE ENGLISH PURPOSES.

HERE COMES ANCIENT *PISTOL*, AND HIS WIFE. -- GOOD CORPORAL, BE *PATIENT* HERE.

HOW NOW, MINE HOST PISTOL?

BASE TIKE, CALL'ST THOU ME *HOST*? NOW, BY THIS HAND I SWEAR, I *SCORN* THE TERM; NOR SHALL MY *NELL* KEEP LODGERS.

NO, BY MY TROTH, NOT LONG: FOR WE CANNOT LODGE AND BOARD A DOZEN OR FOURTEEN GENTLEWOMEN, THAT LIVE HONESTLY BY THE PRICK OF THEIR NEEDLES, BUT IT WILL BE THOUGHT WE KEEP A *BAWDY-HOUSE* STRAIGHT.

O *WELL-A-DAY*, LADY! IF HE BE NOT *DRAWN!* NOW WE SHALL SEE *WILFUL ADULTERY* AND *MURDER* COMMITTED.

GOOD *LIEUTENANT!* GOOD *CORPORAL!* OFFER NOTHING HERE.

PISH!

PISH FOR *THEE*, ICELAND DOG! THOU PRICK-EAR'D *CUR* OF ICELAND!

GOOD CORPORAL NYM, SHOW THY *VALOUR*, AND PUT UP YOUR *SWORD*.

WILL YOU *SHOG OFF?*

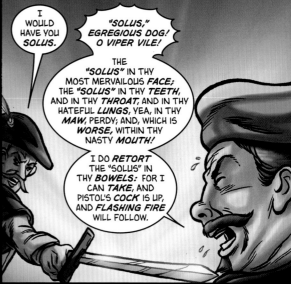

I WOULD HAVE YOU *SOLUS*.

"SOLUS," EGREGIOUS DOG! O VIPER VILE! THE "SOLUS" IN THY MOST MERVAILOUS *FACE;* THE "SOLUS" IN THY *TEETH,* AND IN THY *THROAT,* AND IN THY HATEFUL *LUNGS,* YEA, IN THY *MAW,* PERDY; AND, WHICH IS *WORSE,* WITHIN THY NASTY *MOUTH!*

I DO *RETORT* THE "SOLUS" IN THY *BOWELS:* FOR I CAN *TAKE,* AND PISTOL'S *COCK* IS UP, AND *FLASHING FIRE* WILL FOLLOW.

22

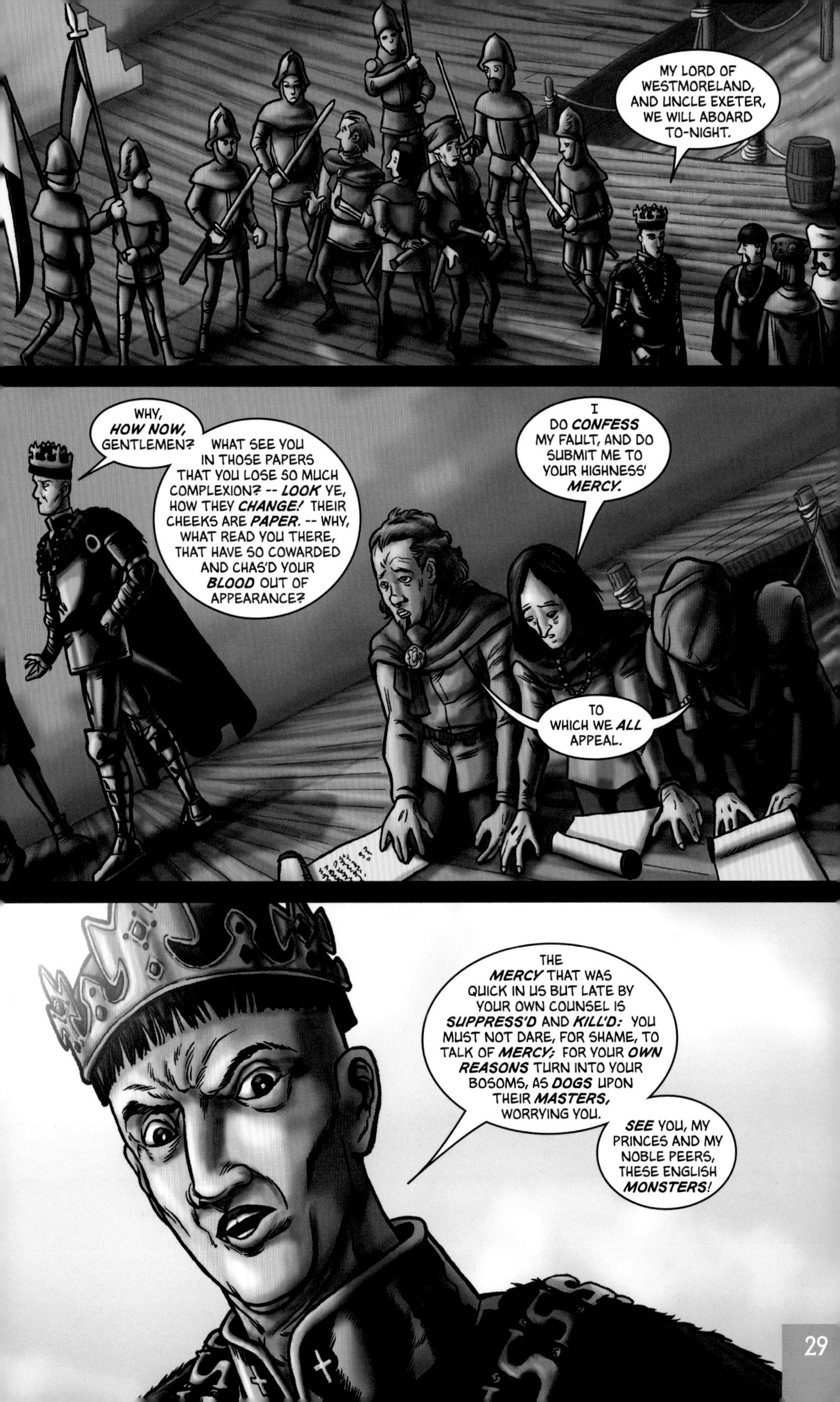
MY LORD OF WESTMORELAND, AND UNCLE EXETER, WE WILL ABOARD TO-NIGHT.
WHY, HOW NOW, GENTLEMEN? WHAT SEE YOU IN THOSE PAPERS THAT YOU LOSE SO MUCH COMPLEXION? -- LOOK YE, HOW THEY CHANGE! THEIR CHEEKS ARE PAPER. -- WHY, WHAT READ YOU THERE, THAT HAVE SO COWARDED AND CHAS'D YOUR BLOOD OUT OF APPEARANCE?
I DO CONFESS MY FAULT, AND DO SUBMIT ME TO YOUR HIGHNESS' MERCY.
TO WHICH WE ALL APPEAL.
THE MERCY THAT WAS QUICK IN US BUT LATE BY YOUR OWN COUNSEL IS SUPPRESS'D AND KILL'D: YOU MUST NOT DARE, FOR SHAME, TO TALK OF MERCY; FOR YOUR OWN REASONS TURN INTO YOUR BOSOMS, AS DOGS UPON THEIR MASTERS, WORRYING YOU.
SEE YOU, MY PRINCES AND MY NOBLE PEERS, THESE ENGLISH MONSTERS!

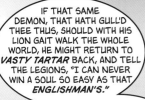

IF THAT SAME DEMON, THAT HATH GULL'D THEE THUS, SHOULD WITH HIS LION GAIT WALK THE WHOLE WORLD, HE MIGHT RETURN TO *VASTY TARTAR* BACK, AND TELL THE LEGIONS, "I CAN NEVER WIN A SOUL SO EASY AS THAT *ENGLISHMAN'S.*"

O, HOW HAST THOU WITH JEALOUSY INFECTED THE *SWEETNESS* OF *AFFIANCE!* SHOW MEN DUTIFUL?

WHY, *SO DIDST THOU:* SEEM THEY GRAVE AND LEARNED? WHY, *SO DIDST THOU:* COME THEY OF NOBLE FAMILY? WHY, *SO DIDST THOU:* SEEM THEY RELIGIOUS? WHY, *SO DIDST THOU:*

OR ARE THEY *SPARE* IN DIET; FREE FROM GROSS PASSION, OR OF MIRTH, OR ANGER; CONSTANT IN SPIRIT, NOT SWERVING WITH THE BLOOD; GARNISH'D AND DECK'D IN MODEST COMPLEMENT, NOT WORKING WITH THE EYE WITHOUT THE EAR, AND BUT IN PURGED JUDGMENT TRUSTING *NEITHER?*

SUCH, AND SO FINELY BOLTED, DIDST *THOU* SEEM; AND THUS THY *FALL* HATH LEFT A KIND OF *BLOT,* TO MARK THE FULL-FRAUGHT MAN AND BEST INDUED, WITH SOME SUSPICION. I WILL *WEEP* FOR THEE;

FOR THIS *REVOLT* OF THINE, METHINKS, IS LIKE ANOTHER FALL OF *MAN.*

THEIR *FAULTS* ARE *OPEN:*

ARREST THEM TO THE ANSWER OF THE LAW; AND *GOD* ACQUIT THEM OF THEIR *PRACTISES!*

I *ARREST* THEE OF *HIGH TREASON,* BY THE NAME OF *RICHARD EARL OF CAMBRIDGE.*

I *ARREST* THEE OF *HIGH TREASON,* BY THE NAME OF *HENRY LORD SCROOP OF MASHAM.*

I *ARREST* THEE OF *HIGH TREASON,* BY THE NAME OF *THOMAS GREY, KNIGHT, OF NORTHUMBERLAND.*

OUR PURPOSES GOD JUSTLY HATH DISCOVER'D, AND I REPENT MY *FAULT* MORE THAN MY *DEATH,* WHICH I BESEECH YOUR HIGHNESS TO FORGIVE, ALTHOUGH MY *BODY* PAY THE PRICE OF IT.

FOR ME, -- THE *GOLD* OF *FRANCE* DID NOT SEDUCE, ALTHOUGH I DID ADMIT IT AS A *MOTIVE,* THE SOONER TO EFFECT WHAT I INTENDED. BUT GOD BE THANKED FOR PREVENTION; WHICH I IN SUFFERANCE HEARTILY WILL REJOICE, BESEECHING *GOD* AND *YOU* TO PARDON ME.

NEVER DID FAITHFUL SUBJECT MORE REJOICE AT THE DISCOVERY OF MOST DANGEROUS TREASON, THAN *I* DO AT THIS HOUR JOY O'ER MYSELF, PREVENTED FROM A *DAMNED* ENTERPRISE. MY *FAULT,* BUT NOT MY *BODY, PARDON,* SOVEREIGN.

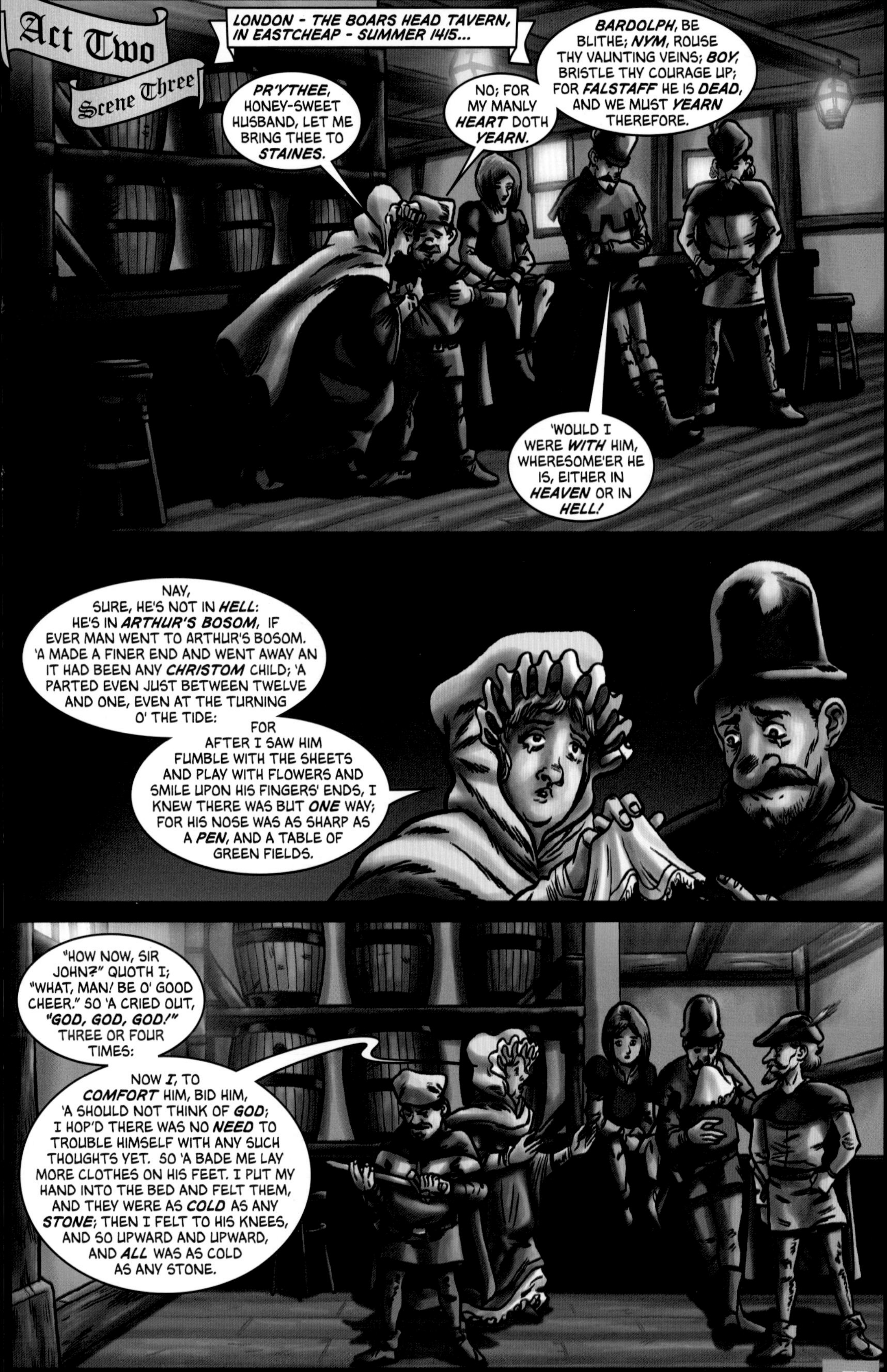

Act Two
Scene Three
LONDON - THE BOARS HEAD TAVERN, IN EASTCHEAP - SUMMER 1415...
PR'YTHEE, HONEY-SWEET HUSBAND, LET ME BRING THEE TO STAINES.
NO; FOR MY MANLY HEART DOTH YEARN.
BARDOLPH, BE BLITHE; NYM, ROUSE THY VAUNTING VEINS; BOY, BRISTLE THY COURAGE UP; FOR FALSTAFF HE IS DEAD, AND WE MUST YEARN THEREFORE.
'WOULD I WERE WITH HIM, WHERESOME'ER HE IS, EITHER IN HEAVEN OR IN HELL!
NAY, SURE, HE'S NOT IN HELL: HE'S IN ARTHUR'S BOSOM, IF EVER MAN WENT TO ARTHUR'S BOSOM. 'A MADE A FINER END AND WENT AWAY AN IT HAD BEEN ANY CHRISTOM CHILD; 'A PARTED EVEN JUST BETWEEN TWELVE AND ONE, EVEN AT THE TURNING O' THE TIDE:
FOR AFTER I SAW HIM FUMBLE WITH THE SHEETS AND PLAY WITH FLOWERS AND SMILE UPON HIS FINGERS' ENDS, I KNEW THERE WAS BUT ONE WAY; FOR HIS NOSE WAS AS SHARP AS A PEN, AND A TABLE OF GREEN FIELDS.
"HOW NOW, SIR JOHN?" QUOTH I; "WHAT, MAN! BE O' GOOD CHEER." SO 'A CRIED OUT, "GOD, GOD, GOD!" THREE OR FOUR TIMES:
NOW I, TO COMFORT HIM, BID HIM, 'A SHOULD NOT THINK OF GOD; I HOP'D THERE WAS NO NEED TO TROUBLE HIMSELF WITH ANY SUCH THOUGHTS YET. SO 'A BADE ME LAY MORE CLOTHES ON HIS FEET. I PUT MY HAND INTO THE BED AND FELT THEM, AND THEY WERE AS COLD AS ANY STONE; THEN I FELT TO HIS KNEES, AND SO UPWARD AND UPWARD, AND ALL WAS AS COLD AS ANY STONE.

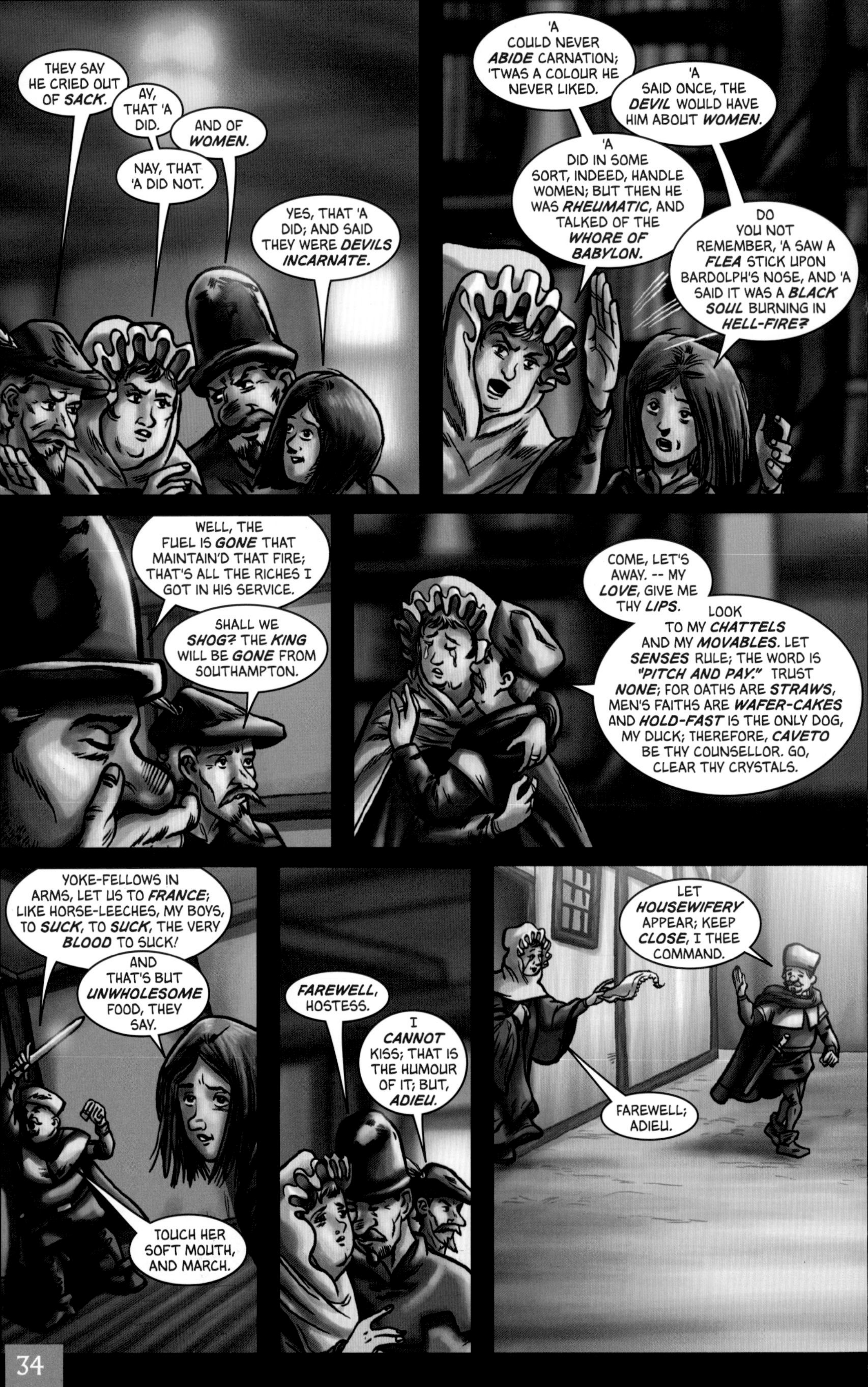
THEY SAY HE CRIED OUT OF SACK.
AY, THAT 'A DID.
AND OF WOMEN.
NAY, THAT 'A DID NOT.
YES, THAT 'A DID; AND SAID THEY WERE DEVILS INCARNATE.
'A COULD NEVER ABIDE CARNATION; 'TWAS A COLOUR HE NEVER LIKED.
'A SAID ONCE, THE DEVIL WOULD HAVE HIM ABOUT WOMEN.
'A DID IN SOME SORT, INDEED, HANDLE WOMEN; BUT THEN HE WAS RHEUMATIC, AND TALKED OF THE WHORE OF BABYLON.
DO YOU NOT REMEMBER, 'A SAW A FLEA STICK UPON BARDOLPH'S NOSE, AND 'A SAID IT WAS A BLACK SOUL BURNING IN HELL-FIRE?
WELL, THE FUEL IS GONE THAT MAINTAIN'D THAT FIRE; THAT'S ALL THE RICHES I GOT IN HIS SERVICE.
SHALL WE SHOG? THE KING WILL BE GONE FROM SOUTHAMPTON.
COME, LET'S AWAY. -- MY LOVE, GIVE ME THY LIPS.
LOOK TO MY CHATTELS AND MY MOVABLES. LET SENSES RULE; THE WORD IS "PITCH AND PAY." TRUST NONE; FOR OATHS ARE STRAWS, MEN'S FAITHS ARE WAFER-CAKES AND HOLD-FAST IS THE ONLY DOG, MY DUCK; THEREFORE, CAVETO BE THY COUNSELLOR. GO, CLEAR THY CRYSTALS.
YOKE-FELLOWS IN ARMS, LET US TO FRANCE; LIKE HORSE-LEECHES, MY BOYS, TO SUCK, TO SUCK, THE VERY BLOOD TO SUCK!
AND THAT'S BUT UNWHOLESOME FOOD, THEY SAY.
TOUCH HER SOFT MOUTH, AND MARCH.
FAREWELL, HOSTESS.
I CANNOT KISS; THAT IS THE HUMOUR OF IT; BUT, ADIEU.
LET HOUSEWIFERY APPEAR; KEEP CLOSE, I THEE COMMAND.
FAREWELL; ADIEU.

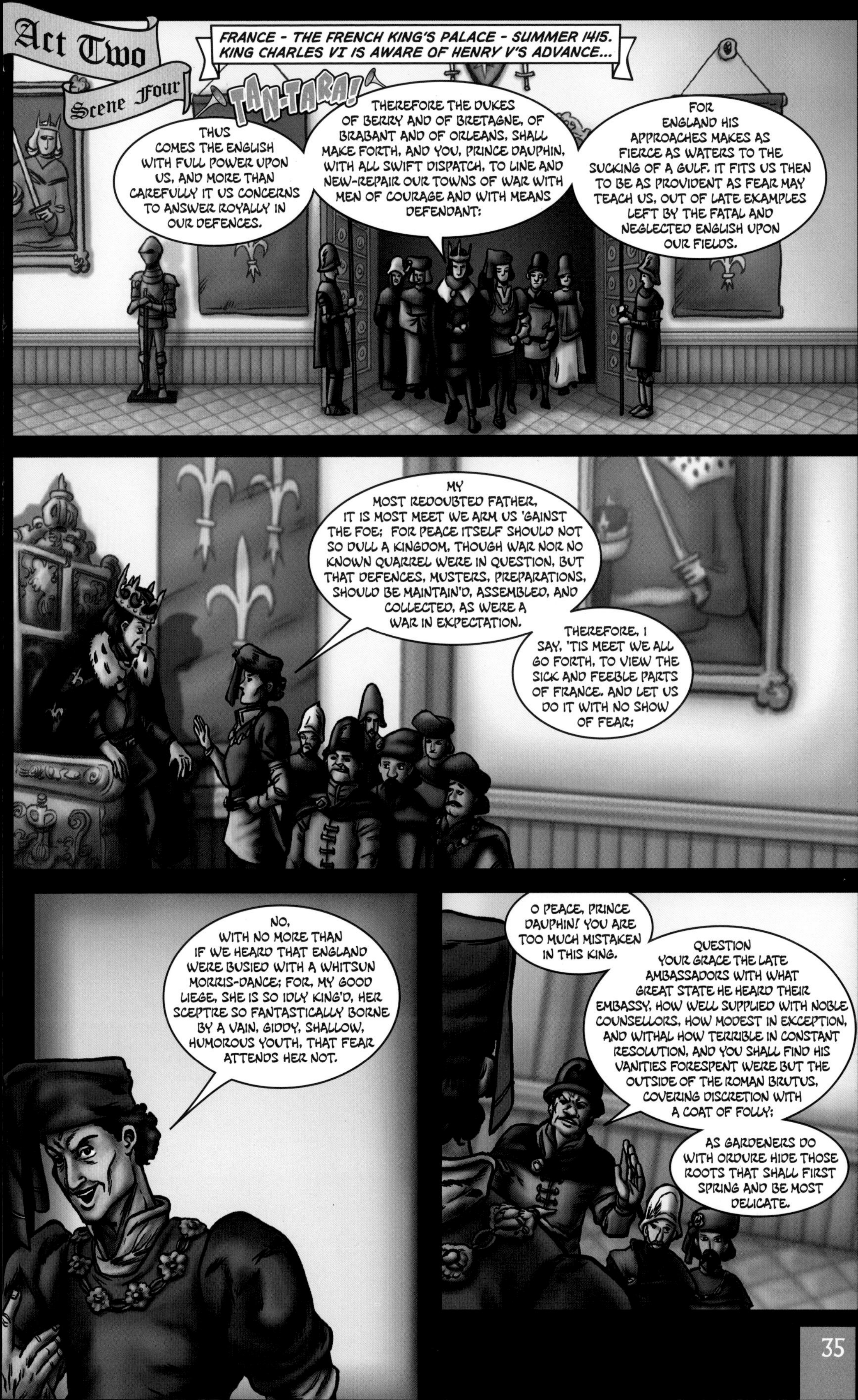
Act Two
Scene Four
FRANCE - THE FRENCH KING'S PALACE - SUMMER 1415. KING CHARLES VI IS AWARE OF HENRY V'S ADVANCE...
TAN-TARA!
THUS COMES THE ENGLISH WITH FULL POWER UPON US, AND MORE THAN CAREFULLY IT US CONCERNS TO ANSWER ROYALLY IN OUR DEFENCES.
THEREFORE THE DUKES OF BERRY AND OF BRETAGNE, OF BRABANT AND OF ORLEANS, SHALL MAKE FORTH, AND YOU, PRINCE DAUPHIN, WITH ALL SWIFT DISPATCH, TO LINE AND NEW-REPAIR OUR TOWNS OF WAR WITH MEN OF COURAGE AND WITH MEANS DEFENDANT:
FOR ENGLAND HIS APPROACHES MAKES AS FIERCE AS WATERS TO THE SUCKING OF A GULF. IT FITS US THEN TO BE AS PROVIDENT AS FEAR MAY TEACH US, OUT OF LATE EXAMPLES LEFT BY THE FATAL AND NEGLECTED ENGLISH UPON OUR FIELDS.
MY MOST REDOUBTED FATHER, IT IS MOST MEET WE ARM US 'GAINST THE FOE; FOR PEACE ITSELF SHOULD NOT SO DULL A KINGDOM, THOUGH WAR NOR NO KNOWN QUARREL WERE IN QUESTION, BUT THAT DEFENCES, MUSTERS, PREPARATIONS, SHOULD BE MAINTAIN'D, ASSEMBLED, AND COLLECTED, AS WERE A WAR IN EXPECTATION.
THEREFORE, I SAY, 'TIS MEET WE ALL GO FORTH, TO VIEW THE SICK AND FEEBLE PARTS OF FRANCE. AND LET US DO IT WITH NO SHOW OF FEAR;
NO, WITH NO MORE THAN IF WE HEARD THAT ENGLAND WERE BUSIED WITH A WHITSUN MORRIS-DANCE; FOR, MY GOOD LIEGE, SHE IS SO IDLY KING'D, HER SCEPTRE SO FANTASTICALLY BORNE BY A VAIN, GIDDY, SHALLOW, HUMOROUS YOUTH, THAT FEAR ATTENDS HER NOT.
O PEACE, PRINCE DAUPHIN! YOU ARE TOO MUCH MISTAKEN IN THIS KING.
QUESTION YOUR GRACE THE LATE AMBASSADORS WITH WHAT GREAT STATE HE HEARD THEIR EMBASSY, HOW WELL SUPPLIED WITH NOBLE COUNSELLORS, HOW MODEST IN EXCEPTION, AND WITHAL HOW TERRIBLE IN CONSTANT RESOLUTION, AND YOU SHALL FIND HIS VANITIES FORESPENT WERE BUT THE OUTSIDE OF THE ROMAN BRUTUS, COVERING DISCRETION WITH A COAT OF FOLLY;
AS GARDENERS DO WITH ORDURE HIDE THOSE ROOTS THAT SHALL FIRST SPRING AND BE MOST DELICATE.

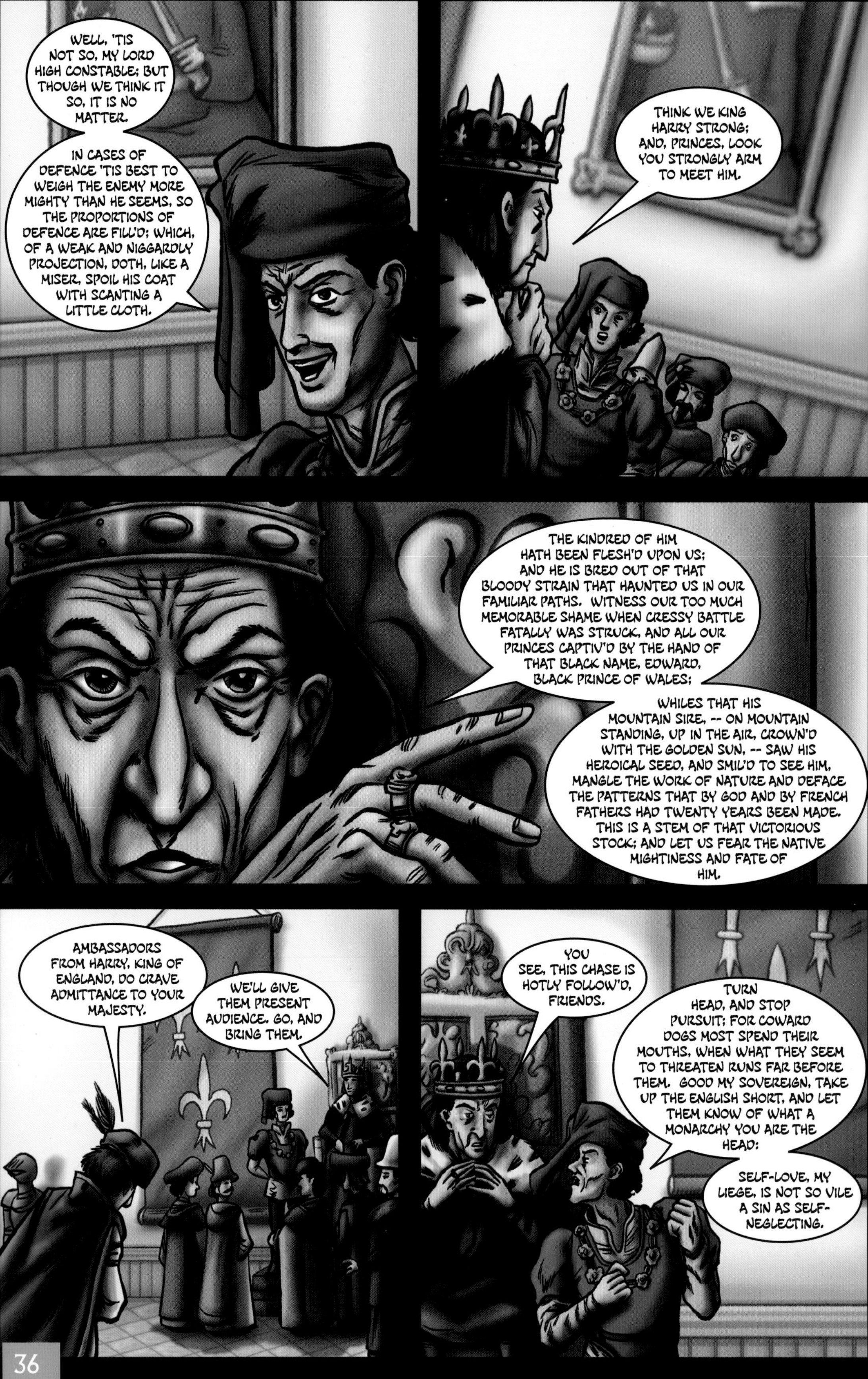
WELL, 'TIS NOT SO, MY LORD HIGH CONSTABLE; BUT THOUGH WE THINK IT SO, IT IS NO MATTER.
IN CASES OF DEFENCE 'TIS BEST TO WEIGH THE ENEMY MORE MIGHTY THAN HE SEEMS, SO THE PROPORTIONS OF DEFENCE ARE FILL'D; WHICH, OF A WEAK AND NIGGARDLY PROJECTION, DOTH, LIKE A MISER, SPOIL HIS COAT WITH SCANTING A LITTLE CLOTH.
THINK WE KING HARRY STRONG; AND, PRINCES, LOOK YOU STRONGLY ARM TO MEET HIM.
THE KINDRED OF HIM HATH BEEN FLESH'D UPON US; AND HE IS BRED OUT OF THAT BLOODY STRAIN THAT HAUNTED US IN OUR FAMILIAR PATHS. WITNESS OUR TOO MUCH MEMORABLE SHAME WHEN CRESSY BATTLE FATALLY WAS STRUCK, AND ALL OUR PRINCES CAPTIV'D BY THE HAND OF THAT BLACK NAME, EDWARD, BLACK PRINCE OF WALES;
WHILES THAT HIS MOUNTAIN SIRE, -- ON MOUNTAIN STANDING, UP IN THE AIR, CROWN'D WITH THE GOLDEN SUN, -- SAW HIS HEROICAL SEED, AND SMIL'D TO SEE HIM, MANGLE THE WORK OF NATURE AND DEFACE THE PATTERNS THAT BY GOD AND BY FRENCH FATHERS HAD TWENTY YEARS BEEN MADE. THIS IS A STEM OF THAT VICTORIOUS STOCK; AND LET US FEAR THE NATIVE MIGHTINESS AND FATE OF HIM.
AMBASSADORS FROM HARRY, KING OF ENGLAND, DO CRAVE ADMITTANCE TO YOUR MAJESTY.
WE'LL GIVE THEM PRESENT AUDIENCE. GO, AND BRING THEM.
YOU SEE, THIS CHASE IS HOTLY FOLLOW'D, FRIENDS.
TURN HEAD, AND STOP PURSUIT; FOR COWARD DOGS MOST SPEND THEIR MOUTHS, WHEN WHAT THEY SEEM TO THREATEN RUNS FAR BEFORE THEM. GOOD MY SOVEREIGN, TAKE UP THE ENGLISH SHORT, AND LET THEM KNOW OF WHAT A MONARCHY YOU ARE THE HEAD:
SELF-LOVE, MY LIEGE, IS NOT SO VILE A SIN AS SELF-NEGLECTING.

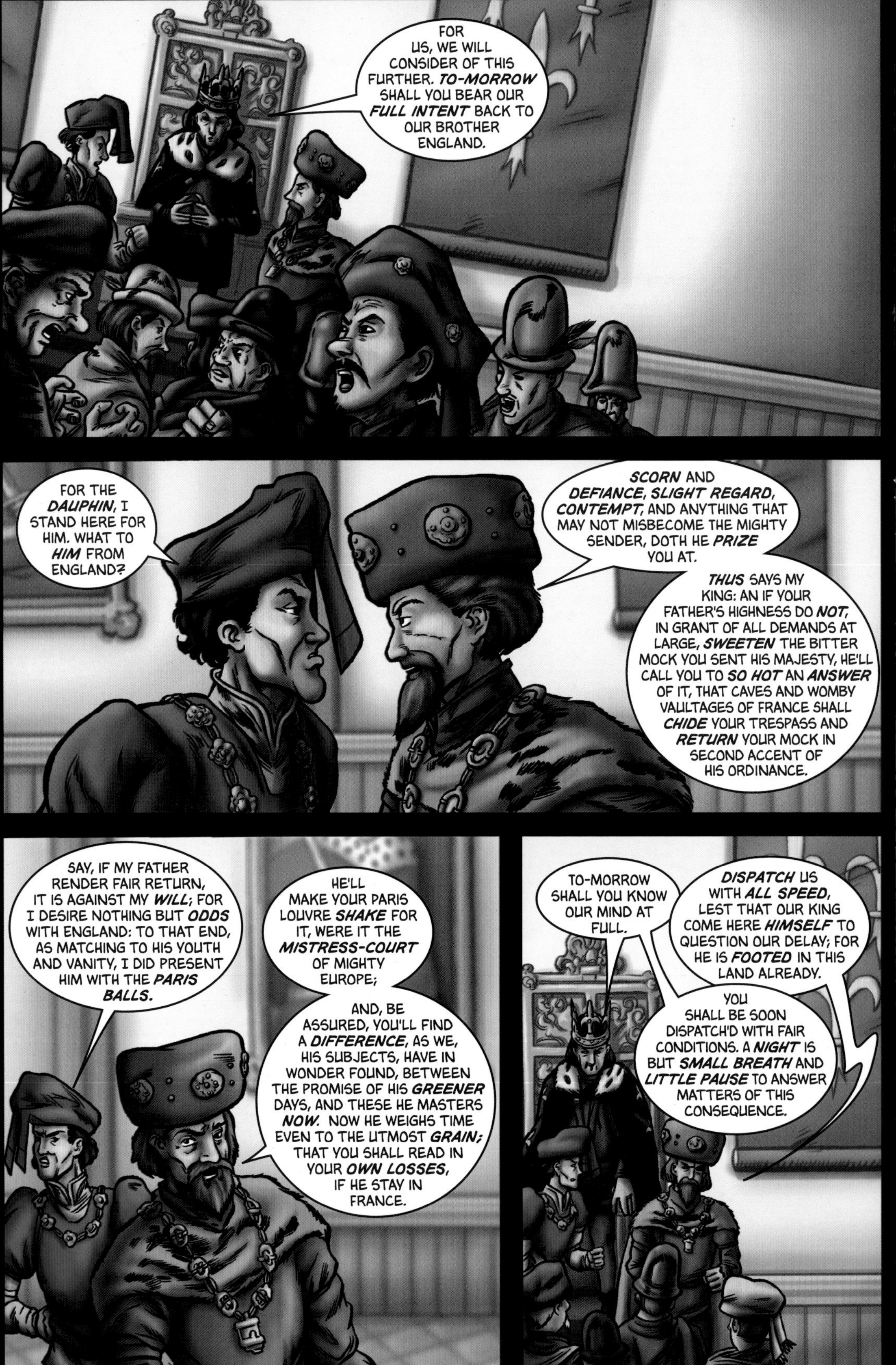
FOR US, WE WILL CONSIDER OF THIS FURTHER. TO-MORROW SHALL YOU BEAR OUR FULL INTENT BACK TO OUR BROTHER ENGLAND.
FOR THE DAUPHIN, I STAND HERE FOR HIM. WHAT TO HIM FROM ENGLAND?
SCORN AND DEFIANCE, SLIGHT REGARD, CONTEMPT, AND ANYTHING THAT MAY NOT MISBECOME THE MIGHTY SENDER, DOTH HE PRIZE YOU AT.
THUS SAYS MY KING: AN IF YOUR FATHER'S HIGHNESS DO NOT, IN GRANT OF ALL DEMANDS AT LARGE, SWEETEN THE BITTER MOCK YOU SENT HIS MAJESTY, HE'LL CALL YOU TO SO HOT AN ANSWER OF IT, THAT CAVES AND WOMBY VAULTAGES OF FRANCE SHALL CHIDE YOUR TRESPASS AND RETURN YOUR MOCK IN SECOND ACCENT OF HIS ORDINANCE.
SAY, IF MY FATHER RENDER FAIR RETURN, IT IS AGAINST MY WILL; FOR I DESIRE NOTHING BUT ODDS WITH ENGLAND: TO THAT END, AS MATCHING TO HIS YOUTH AND VANITY, I DID PRESENT HIM WITH THE PARIS BALLS.
HE'LL MAKE YOUR PARIS LOUVRE SHAKE FOR IT, WERE IT THE MISTRESS-COURT OF MIGHTY EUROPE;
AND, BE ASSURED, YOU'LL FIND A DIFFERENCE, AS WE, HIS SUBJECTS, HAVE IN WONDER FOUND, BETWEEN THE PROMISE OF HIS GREENER DAYS, AND THESE HE MASTERS NOW. NOW HE WEIGHS TIME EVEN TO THE UTMOST GRAIN; THAT YOU SHALL READ IN YOUR OWN LOSSES, IF HE STAY IN FRANCE.
TO-MORROW SHALL YOU KNOW OUR MIND AT FULL.
DISPATCH US WITH ALL SPEED, LEST THAT OUR KING COME HERE HIMSELF TO QUESTION OUR DELAY; FOR HE IS FOOTED IN THIS LAND ALREADY.
YOU SHALL BE SOON DISPATCH'D WITH FAIR CONDITIONS. A NIGHT IS BUT SMALL BREATH AND LITTLE PAUSE TO ANSWER MATTERS OF THIS CONSEQUENCE.

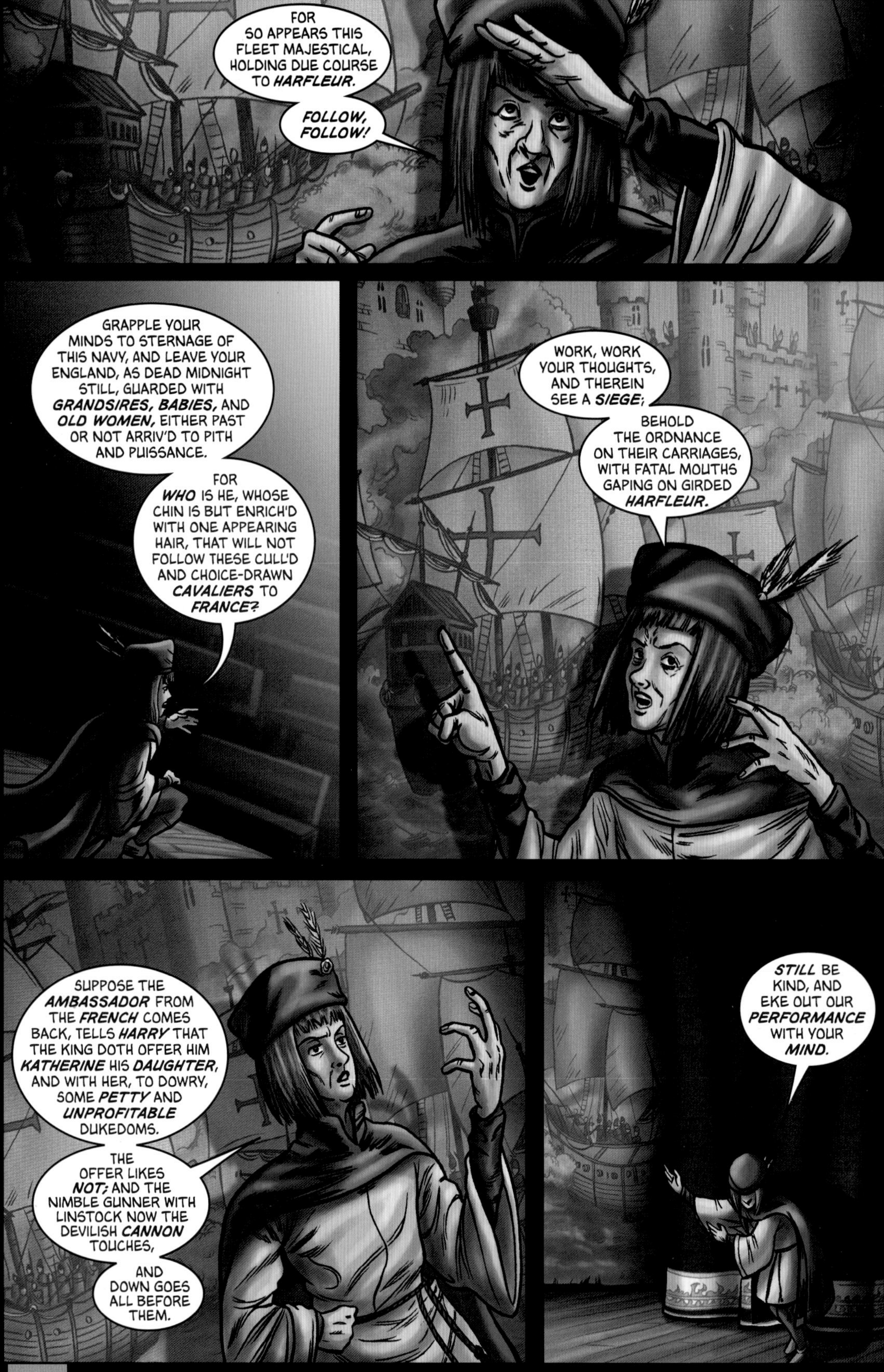
FOR SO APPEARS THIS FLEET MAJESTICAL, HOLDING DUE COURSE TO HARFLEUR.
FOLLOW, FOLLOW!
GRAPPLE YOUR MINDS TO STERNAGE OF THIS NAVY, AND LEAVE YOUR ENGLAND, AS DEAD MIDNIGHT STILL, GUARDED WITH GRANDSIRES, BABIES, AND OLD WOMEN, EITHER PAST OR NOT ARRIV'D TO PITH AND PUISSANCE.
FOR WHO IS HE, WHOSE CHIN IS BUT ENRICH'D WITH ONE APPEARING HAIR, THAT WILL NOT FOLLOW THESE CULL'D AND CHOICE-DRAWN CAVALIERS TO FRANCE?
WORK, WORK YOUR THOUGHTS, AND THEREIN SEE A SIEGE;
BEHOLD THE ORDNANCE ON THEIR CARRIAGES, WITH FATAL MOUTHS GAPING ON GIRDED HARFLEUR.
SUPPOSE THE AMBASSADOR FROM THE FRENCH COMES BACK, TELLS HARRY THAT THE KING DOTH OFFER HIM KATHERINE HIS DAUGHTER, AND WITH HER, TO DOWRY, SOME PETTY AND UNPROFITABLE DUKEDOMS.
THE OFFER LIKES NOT; AND THE NIMBLE GUNNER WITH LINSTOCK NOW THE DEVILISH CANNON TOUCHES,
AND DOWN GOES ALL BEFORE THEM.
STILL BE KIND, AND EKE OUT OUR PERFORMANCE WITH YOUR MIND.

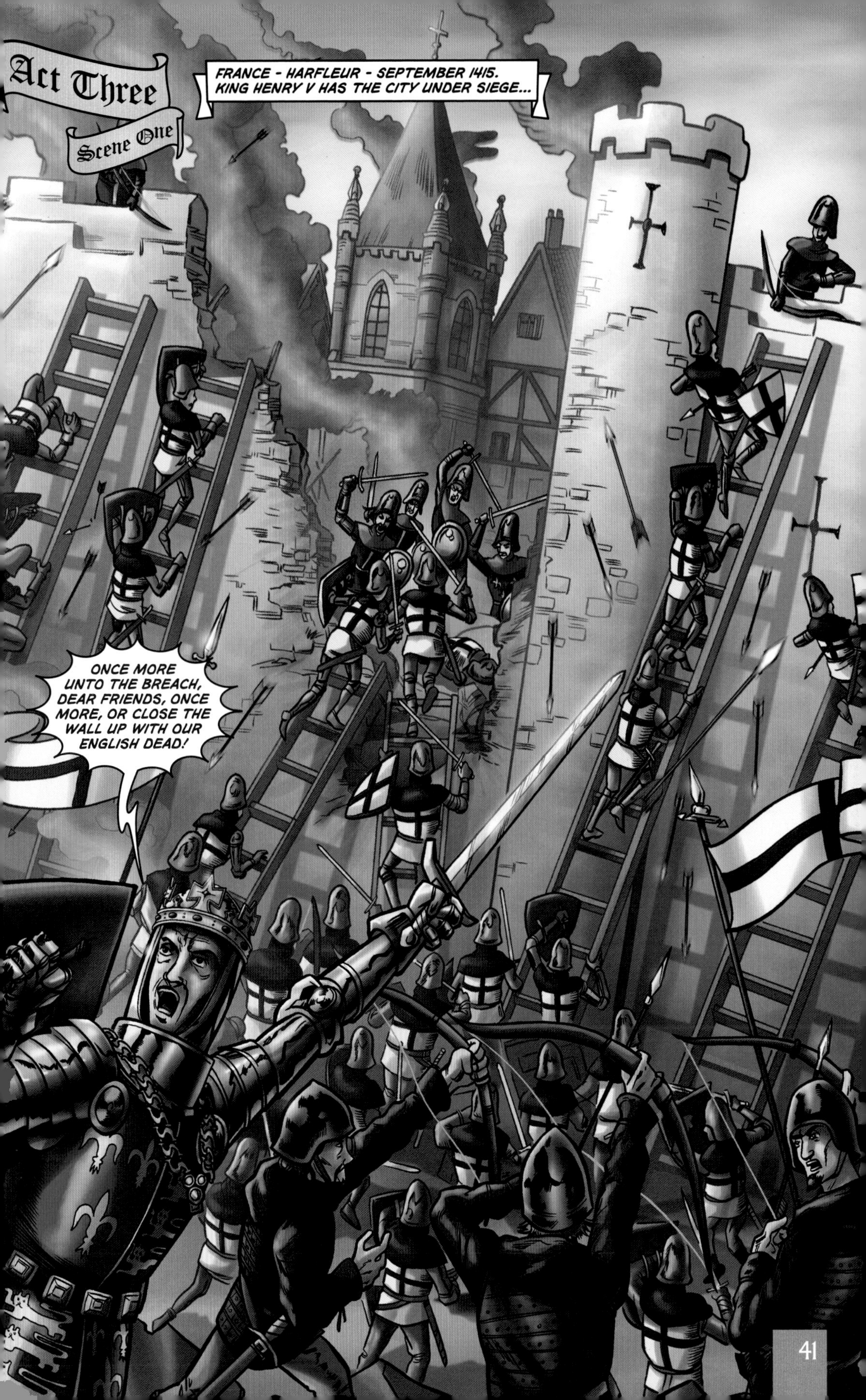
Act Three
Scene One
FRANCE - HARFLEUR - SEPTEMBER 1415.
KING HENRY V HAS THE CITY UNDER SIEGE...
ONCE MORE UNTO THE BREACH, DEAR FRIENDS, ONCE MORE, OR CLOSE THE WALL UP WITH OUR ENGLISH DEAD!

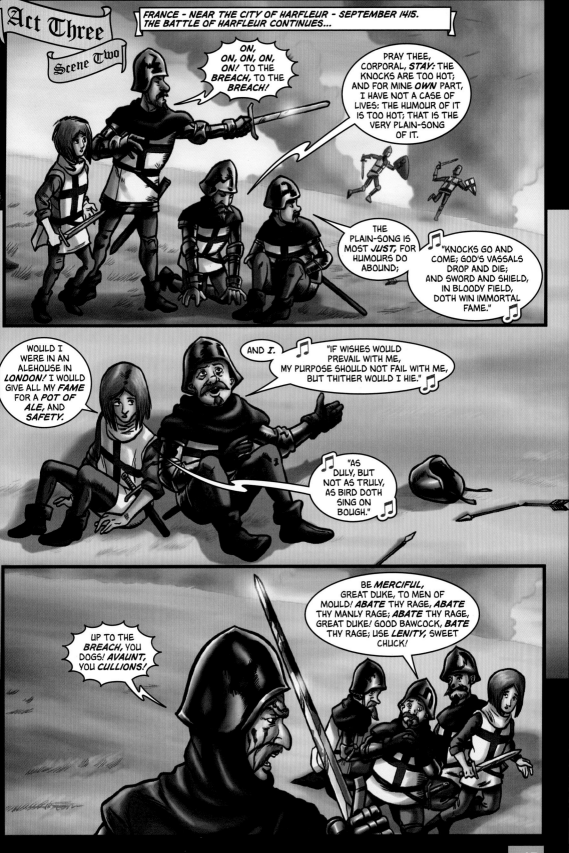

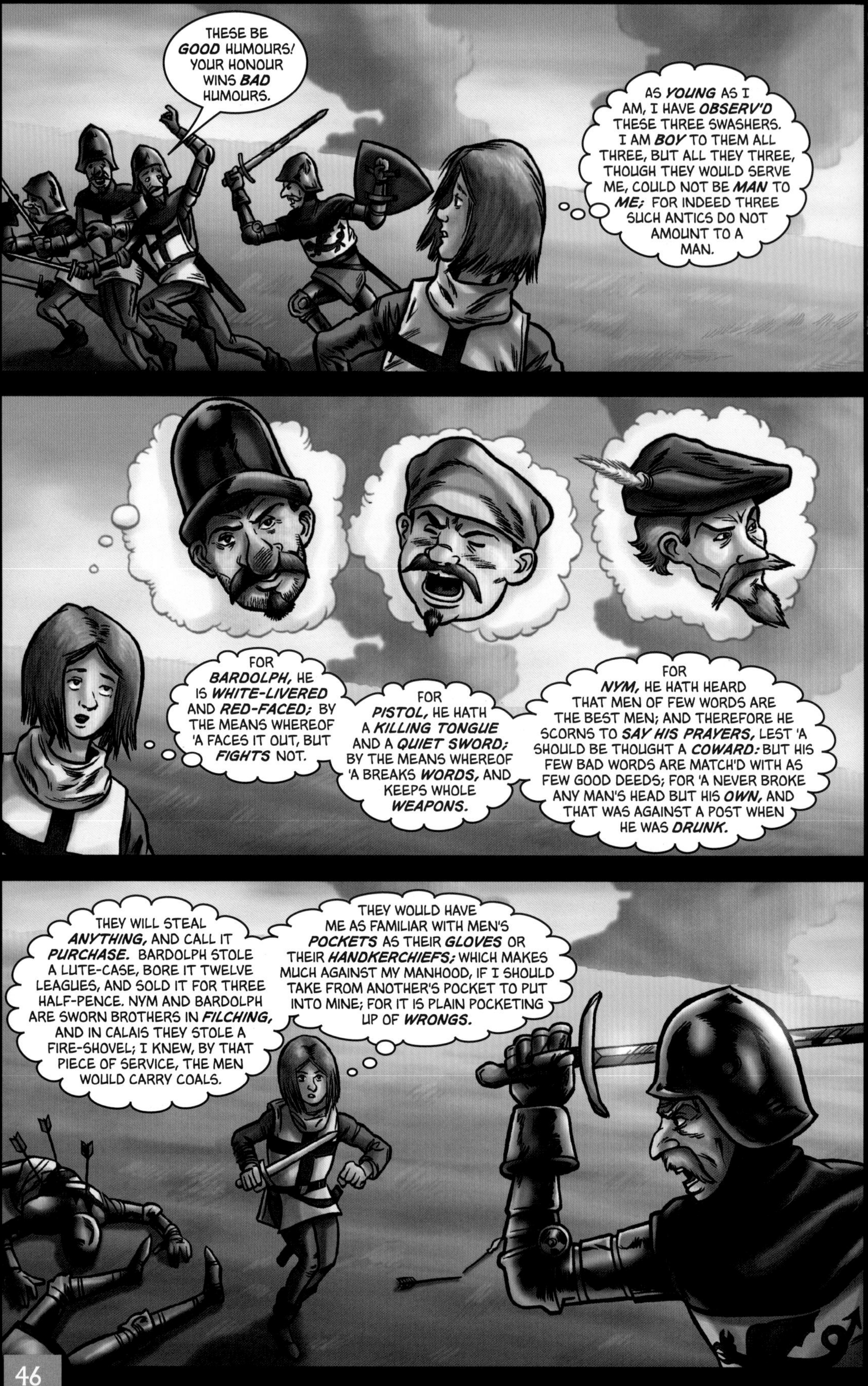
THESE BE GOOD HUMOURS! YOUR HONOUR WINS BAD HUMOURS.
AS YOUNG AS I AM, I HAVE OBSERV'D THESE THREE SWASHERS. I AM BOY TO THEM ALL THREE, BUT ALL THEY THREE, THOUGH THEY WOULD SERVE ME, COULD NOT BE MAN TO ME; FOR INDEED THREE SUCH ANTICS DO NOT AMOUNT TO A MAN.
FOR BARDOLPH, HE IS WHITE-LIVERED AND RED-FACED; BY THE MEANS WHEREOF 'A FACES IT OUT, BUT FIGHTS NOT.
FOR PISTOL, HE HATH A KILLING TONGUE AND A QUIET SWORD; BY THE MEANS WHEREOF 'A BREAKS WORDS, AND KEEPS WHOLE WEAPONS.
FOR NYM, HE HATH HEARD THAT MEN OF FEW WORDS ARE THE BEST MEN; AND THEREFORE HE SCORNS TO SAY HIS PRAYERS, LEST 'A SHOULD BE THOUGHT A COWARD: BUT HIS FEW BAD WORDS ARE MATCH'D WITH AS FEW GOOD DEEDS; FOR 'A NEVER BROKE ANY MAN'S HEAD BUT HIS OWN, AND THAT WAS AGAINST A POST WHEN HE WAS DRUNK.
THEY WILL STEAL ANYTHING, AND CALL IT PURCHASE. BARDOLPH STOLE A LUTE-CASE, BORE IT TWELVE LEAGUES, AND SOLD IT FOR THREE HALF-PENCE. NYM AND BARDOLPH ARE SWORN BROTHERS IN FILCHING, AND IN CALAIS THEY STOLE A FIRE-SHOVEL; I KNEW, BY THAT PIECE OF SERVICE, THE MEN WOULD CARRY COALS.
THEY WOULD HAVE ME AS FAMILIAR WITH MEN'S POCKETS AS THEIR GLOVES OR THEIR HANDKERCHIEFS; WHICH MAKES MUCH AGAINST MY MANHOOD, IF I SHOULD TAKE FROM ANOTHER'S POCKET TO PUT INTO MINE; FOR IT IS PLAIN POCKETING UP OF WRONGS.

49

53

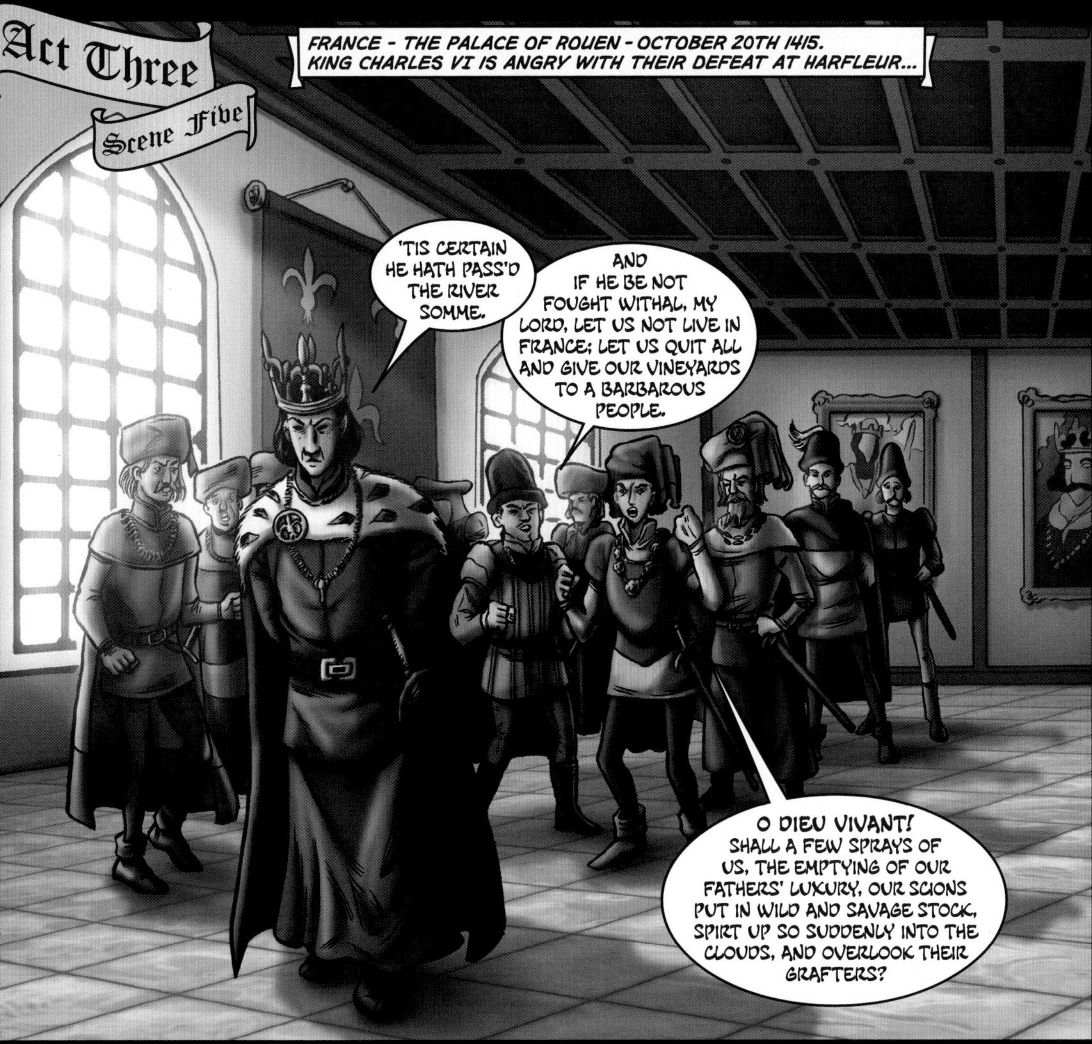
Act Three
Scene Five
FRANCE - THE PALACE OF ROUEN - OCTOBER 20TH 1415. KING CHARLES VI IS ANGRY WITH THEIR DEFEAT AT HARFLEUR...
'TIS CERTAIN HE HATH PASS'D THE RIVER SOMME.
AND IF HE BE NOT FOUGHT WITHAL, MY LORD, LET US NOT LIVE IN FRANCE; LET US QUIT ALL AND GIVE OUR VINEYARDS TO A BARBAROUS PEOPLE.
O DIEU VIVANT! SHALL A FEW SPRAYS OF US, THE EMPTYING OF OUR FATHERS' LUXURY, OUR SCIONS PUT IN WILD AND SAVAGE STOCK, SPIRT UP SO SUDDENLY INTO THE CLOUDS, AND OVERLOOK THEIR GRAFTERS?

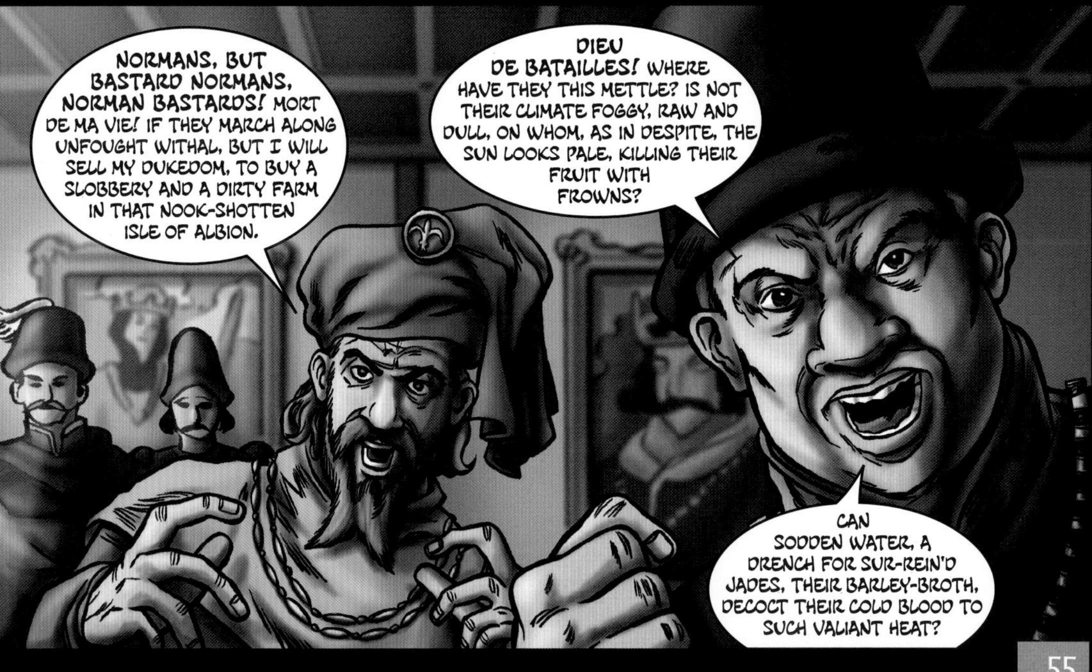
NORMANS, BUT BASTARD NORMANS, NORMAN BASTARDS! MORT DE MA VIE! IF THEY MARCH ALONG UNFOUGHT WITHAL, BUT I WILL SELL MY DUKEDOM, TO BUY A SLOBBERY AND A DIRTY FARM IN THAT NOOK-SHOTTEN ISLE OF ALBION.
DIEU DE BATAILLES! WHERE HAVE THEY THIS METTLE? IS NOT THEIR CLIMATE FOGGY, RAW AND DULL, ON WHOM, AS IN DESPITE, THE SUN LOOKS PALE, KILLING THEIR FRUIT WITH FROWNS?
CAN SODDEN WATER, A DRENCH FOR SUR-REIN'D JADES, THEIR BARLEY-BROTH, DECOCT THEIR COLD BLOOD TO SUCH VALIANT HEAT?

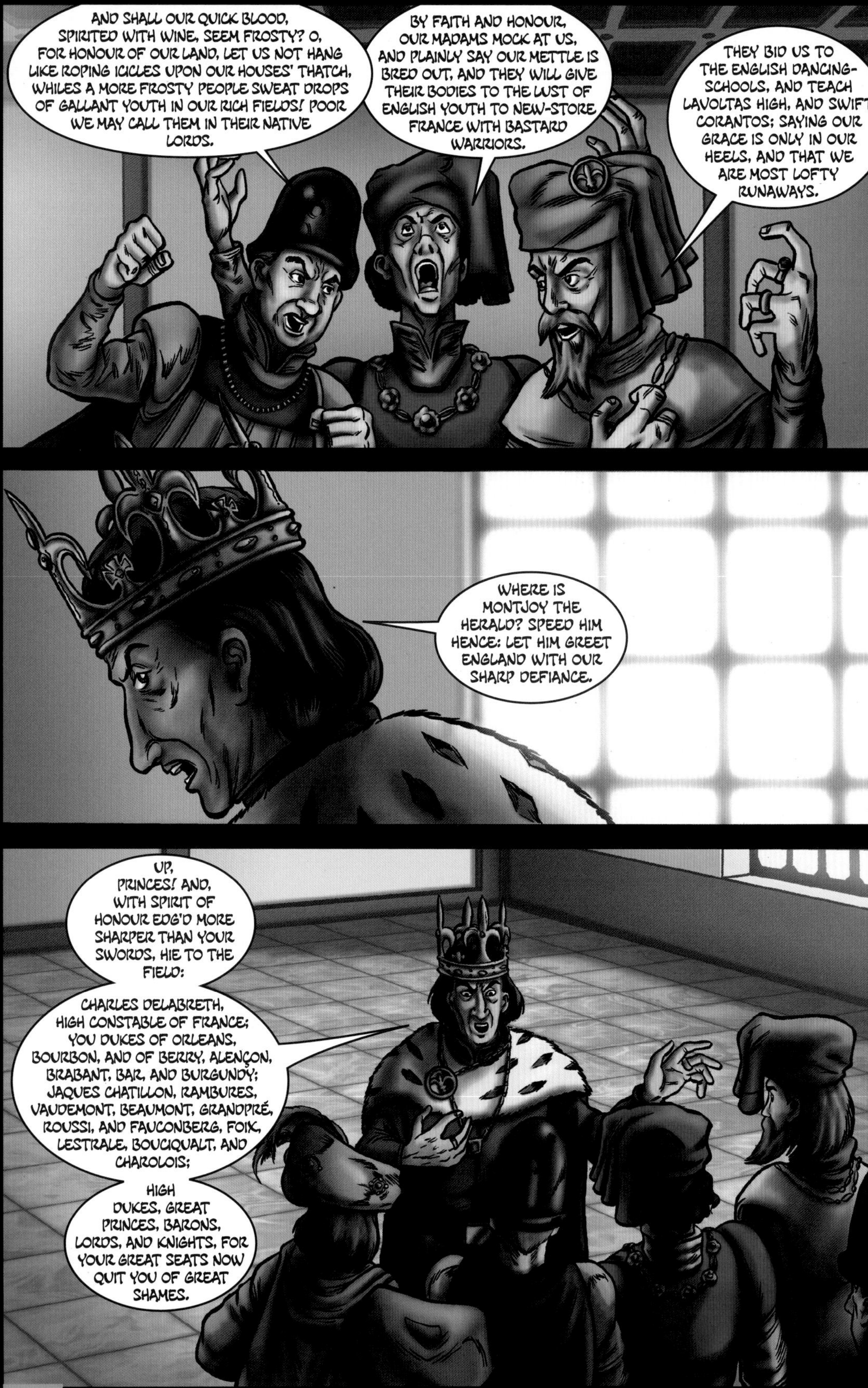
AND SHALL OUR QUICK BLOOD, SPIRITED WITH WINE, SEEM FROSTY? O, FOR HONOUR OF OUR LAND, LET US NOT HANG LIKE ROPING ICICLES UPON OUR HOUSES' THATCH, WHILES A MORE FROSTY PEOPLE SWEAT DROPS OF GALLANT YOUTH IN OUR RICH FIELDS! POOR WE MAY CALL THEM IN THEIR NATIVE LORDS.
BY FAITH AND HONOUR, OUR MADAMS MOCK AT US, AND PLAINLY SAY OUR METTLE IS BRED OUT, AND THEY WILL GIVE THEIR BODIES TO THE LUST OF ENGLISH YOUTH TO NEW-STORE FRANCE WITH BASTARD WARRIORS.
THEY BID US TO THE ENGLISH DANCING-SCHOOLS, AND TEACH LAVOLTAS HIGH, AND SWIFT CORANTOS; SAYING OUR GRACE IS ONLY IN OUR HEELS, AND THAT WE ARE MOST LOFTY RUNAWAYS.
WHERE IS MONTJOY THE HERALD? SPEED HIM HENCE: LET HIM GREET ENGLAND WITH OUR SHARP DEFIANCE.
UP, PRINCES! AND, WITH SPIRIT OF HONOUR EDG'D MORE SHARPER THAN YOUR SWORDS, HIE TO THE FIELD:
CHARLES DELABRETH, HIGH CONSTABLE OF FRANCE; YOU DUKES OF ORLEANS, BOURBON, AND OF BERRY, ALENÇON, BRABANT, BAR, AND BURGUNDY; JAQUES CHATILLON, RAMBURES, VAUDEMONT, BEAUMONT, GRANDPRÉ, ROUSSI, AND FAUCONBERG, FOIX, LESTRALE, BOUCIQUALT, AND CHAROLOIS;
HIGH DUKES, GREAT PRINCES, BARONS, LORDS, AND KNIGHTS, FOR YOUR GREAT SEATS NOW QUIT YOU OF GREAT SHAMES.

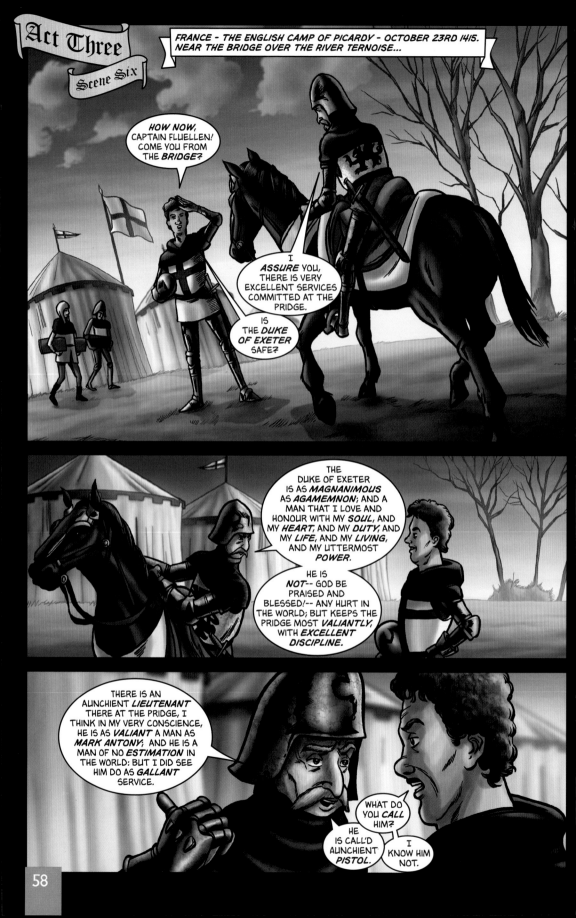

HERE IS THE MAN.

CAPTAIN, I THEE BESEECH TO DO ME FAVOURS: THE DUKE OF EXETER DOTH LOVE THEE WELL.

AY, I PRAISE GOD; AND I HAVE MERITED SOME LOVE AT HIS HANDS.

BARDOLPH, A SOLDIER, FIRM AND SOUND OF HEART, AND OF BUXOM VALOUR, HATH BY CRUEL FATE AND GIDDY FORTUNE'S FURIOUS FICKLE WHEEL, THAT GODDESS BLIND, THAT STANDS UPON THE ROLLING RESTLESS STONE--

BY YOUR PATIENCE, AUNCHIENT PISTOL. FORTUNE IS PAINTED BLIND, WITH A MUFFLER AFORE HER EYES, TO SIGNIFY TO YOU THAT FORTUNE IS BLIND; AND SHE IS PAINTED ALSO WITH A WHEEL, TO SIGNIFY TO YOU, WHICH IS THE MORAL OF IT, THAT SHE IS TURNING, AND INCONSTANT, AND MUTABILITY, AND VARIATION;

AND HER FOOT, LOOK YOU, IS FIXED UPON A SPHERICAL STONE, WHICH ROLLS, AND ROLLS, AND ROLLS. IN GOOD TRUTH, THE POET MAKES A MOST EXCELLENT DESCRIPTION OF IT: FORTUNE IS AN EXCELLENT MORAL.

FORTUNE IS BARDOLPH'S FOE, AND FROWNS ON HIM; FOR HE HATH STOLEN A PAX, AND HANGED MUST 'A BE,-- A DAMNED DEATH!

LET GALLOWS GAPE FOR DOG; LET MAN GO FREE, AND LET NOT HEMP HIS WINDPIPE SUFFOCATE. BUT EXETER HATH GIVEN THE DOOM OF DEATH FOR PAX OF LITTLE PRICE.

THEREFORE, GO SPEAK-- THE DUKE WILL HEAR THY VOICE-- AND LET NOT BARDOLPH'S VITAL THREAD BE CUT WITH EDGE OF PENNY CORD AND VILE REPROACH. SPEAK, CAPTAIN, FOR HIS LIFE, AND I WILL THEE REQUITE.

AUNCHIENT PISTOL, I DO PARTLY UNDERSTAND YOUR MEANING.

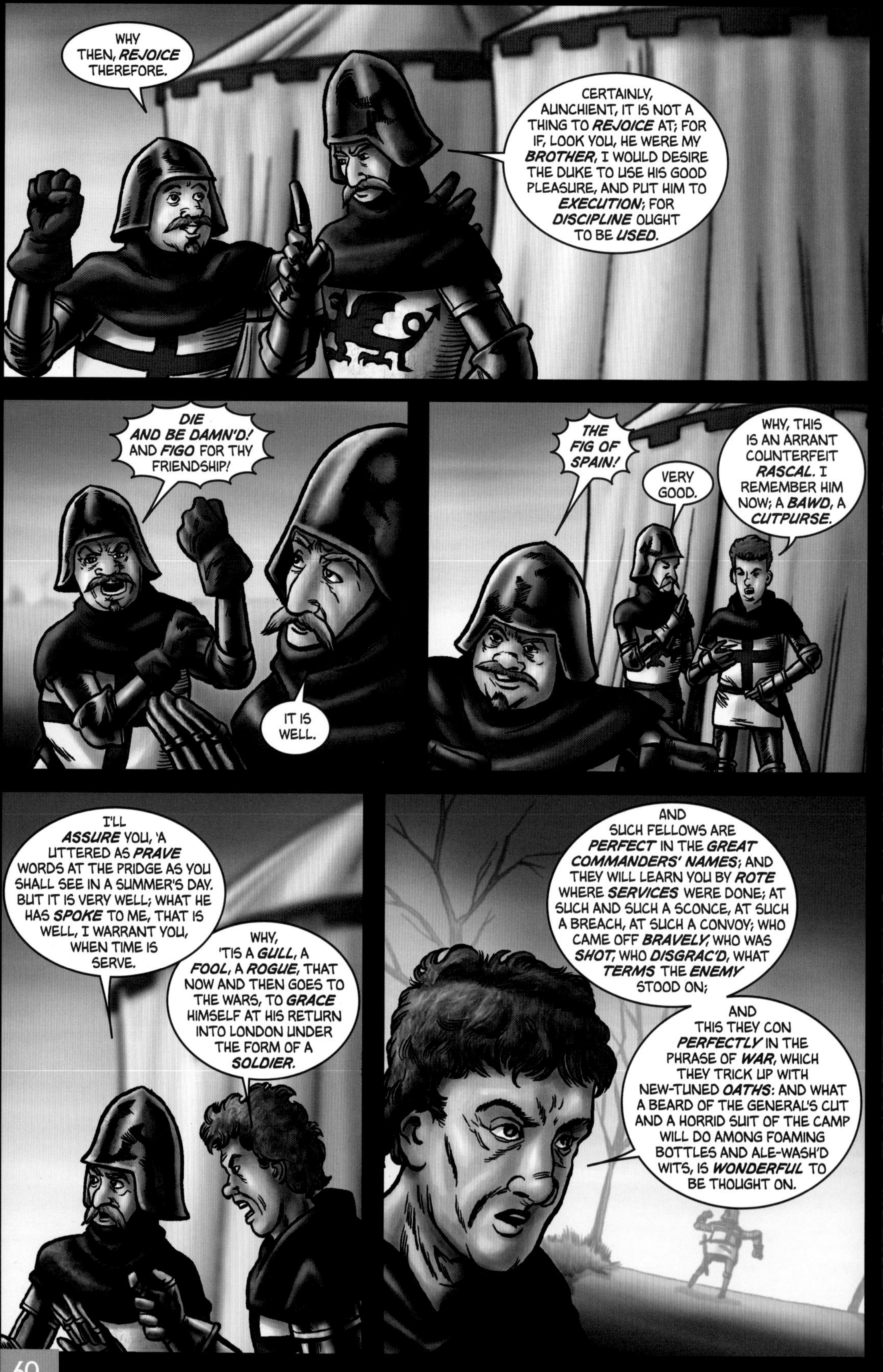
WHY THEN, REJOICE THEREFORE.
CERTAINLY, AUNCHIENT, IT IS NOT A THING TO REJOICE AT; FOR IF, LOOK YOU, HE WERE MY BROTHER, I WOULD DESIRE THE DUKE TO USE HIS GOOD PLEASURE, AND PUT HIM TO EXECUTION; FOR DISCIPLINE OUGHT TO BE USED.
DIE AND BE DAMN'D! AND FIGO FOR THY FRIENDSHIP!
IT IS WELL.
THE FIG OF SPAIN!
VERY GOOD.
WHY, THIS IS AN ARRANT COUNTERFEIT RASCAL. I REMEMBER HIM NOW; A BAWD, A CUTPURSE.
I'LL ASSURE YOU, 'A UTTERED AS PRAVE WORDS AT THE PRIDGE AS YOU SHALL SEE IN A SUMMER'S DAY. BUT IT IS VERY WELL; WHAT HE HAS SPOKE TO ME, THAT IS WELL, I WARRANT YOU, WHEN TIME IS SERVE.
WHY, 'TIS A GULL, A FOOL, A ROGUE, THAT NOW AND THEN GOES TO THE WARS, TO GRACE HIMSELF AT HIS RETURN INTO LONDON UNDER THE FORM OF A SOLDIER.
AND SUCH FELLOWS ARE PERFECT IN THE GREAT COMMANDERS' NAMES; AND THEY WILL LEARN YOU BY ROTE WHERE SERVICES WERE DONE; AT SUCH AND SUCH A SCONCE, AT SUCH A BREACH, AT SUCH A CONVOY; WHO CAME OFF BRAVELY, WHO WAS SHOT, WHO DISGRAC'D, WHAT TERMS THE ENEMY STOOD ON;
AND THIS THEY CON PERFECTLY IN THE PHRASE OF WAR, WHICH THEY TRICK UP WITH NEW-TUNED OATHS: AND WHAT A BEARD OF THE GENERAL'S CUT AND A HORRID SUIT OF THE CAMP WILL DO AMONG FOAMING BOTTLES AND ALE-WASH'D WITS, IS WONDERFUL TO BE THOUGHT ON.

61

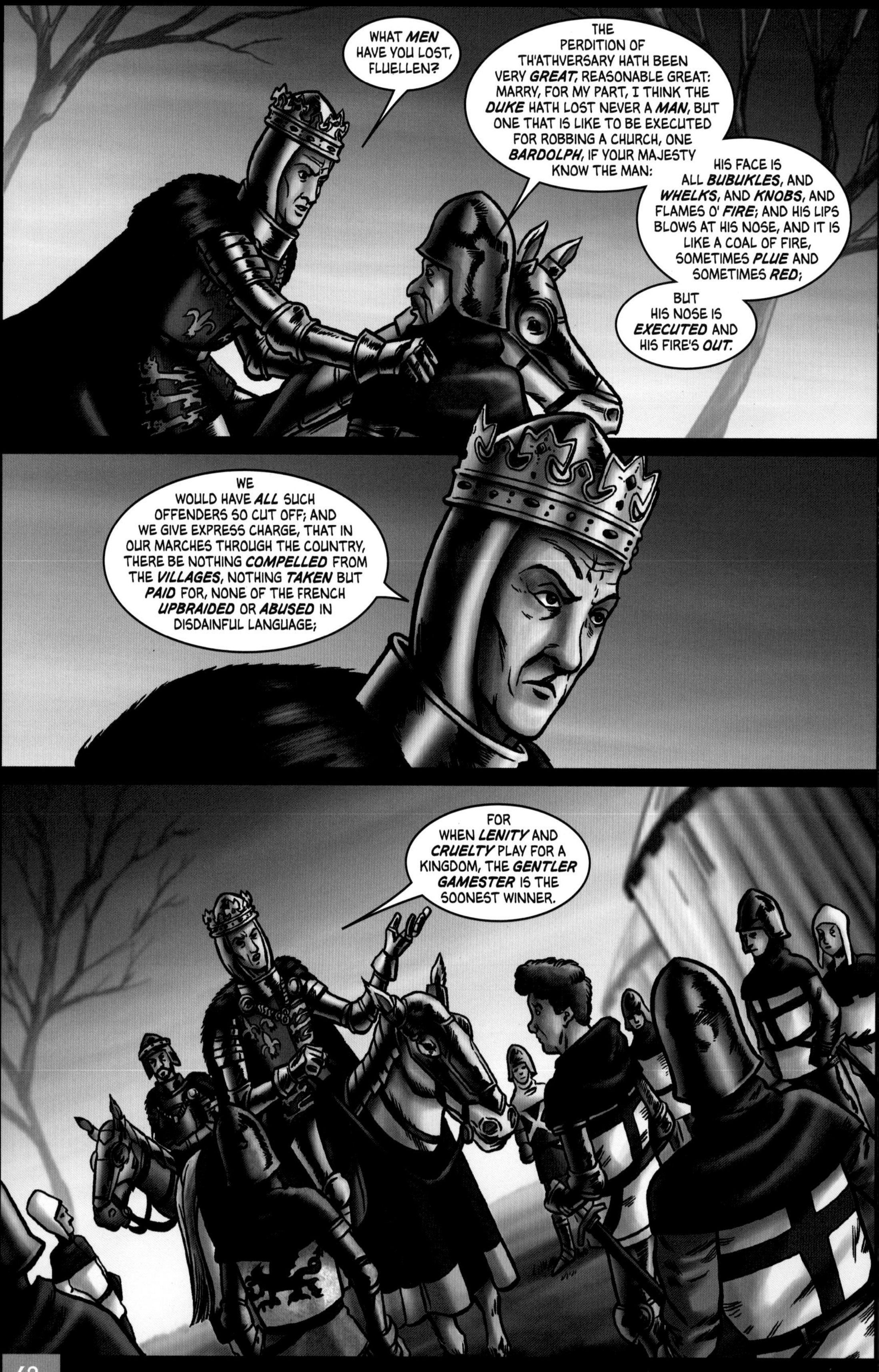
WHAT MEN HAVE YOU LOST, FLUELLEN?
THE PERDITION OF TH'ATHVERSARY HATH BEEN VERY GREAT, REASONABLE GREAT: MARRY, FOR MY PART, I THINK THE DUKE HATH LOST NEVER A MAN, BUT ONE THAT IS LIKE TO BE EXECUTED FOR ROBBING A CHURCH, ONE BARDOLPH, IF YOUR MAJESTY KNOW THE MAN:
HIS FACE IS ALL BUBUKLES, AND WHELKS, AND KNOBS, AND FLAMES O' FIRE; AND HIS LIPS BLOWS AT HIS NOSE, AND IT IS LIKE A COAL OF FIRE, SOMETIMES PLUE AND SOMETIMES RED;
BUT HIS NOSE IS EXECUTED AND HIS FIRE'S OUT.
WE WOULD HAVE ALL SUCH OFFENDERS SO CUT OFF; AND WE GIVE EXPRESS CHARGE, THAT IN OUR MARCHES THROUGH THE COUNTRY, THERE BE NOTHING COMPELLED FROM THE VILLAGES, NOTHING TAKEN BUT PAID FOR, NONE OF THE FRENCH UPBRAIDED OR ABUSED IN DISDAINFUL LANGUAGE;
FOR WHEN LENITY AND CRUELTY PLAY FOR A KINGDOM, THE GENTLER GAMESTER IS THE SOONEST WINNER.

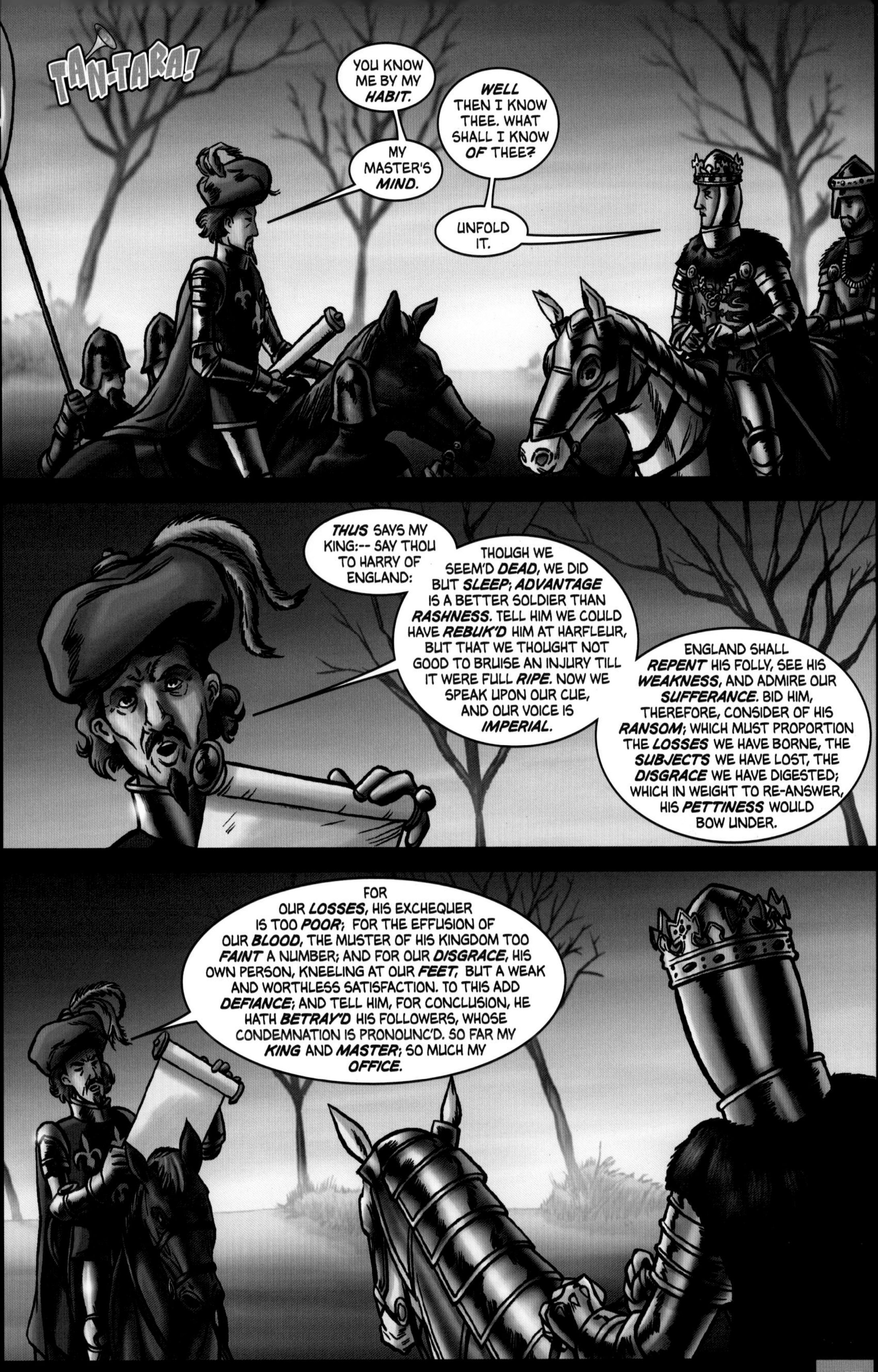
TAN-TARA!
YOU KNOW ME BY MY *HABIT.*
MY MASTER'S *MIND.*
WELL THEN I KNOW THEE. WHAT SHALL I KNOW *OF* THEE?
UNFOLD IT.
THUS SAYS MY KING:-- SAY THOU TO HARRY OF ENGLAND:
THOUGH WE SEEM'D *DEAD,* WE DID BUT *SLEEP; ADVANTAGE* IS A BETTER SOLDIER THAN *RASHNESS.* TELL HIM WE COULD HAVE *REBUK'D* HIM AT HARFLEUR, BUT THAT WE THOUGHT NOT GOOD TO BRUISE AN INJURY TILL IT WERE FULL *RIPE.* NOW WE SPEAK UPON OUR CUE, AND OUR VOICE IS *IMPERIAL.*
ENGLAND SHALL *REPENT* HIS FOLLY, SEE HIS *WEAKNESS,* AND ADMIRE OUR *SUFFERANCE.* BID HIM, THEREFORE, CONSIDER OF HIS *RANSOM;* WHICH MUST PROPORTION THE *LOSSES* WE HAVE BORNE, THE *SUBJECTS* WE HAVE LOST, THE *DISGRACE* WE HAVE DIGESTED; WHICH IN WEIGHT TO RE-ANSWER, HIS *PETTINESS* WOULD BOW UNDER.
FOR OUR *LOSSES,* HIS EXCHEQUER IS TOO *POOR;* FOR THE EFFUSION OF OUR *BLOOD,* THE MUSTER OF HIS KINGDOM TOO *FAINT* A NUMBER; AND FOR OUR *DISGRACE,* HIS OWN PERSON, KNEELING AT OUR *FEET,* BUT A WEAK AND WORTHLESS SATISFACTION. TO THIS ADD *DEFIANCE;* AND TELL HIM, FOR CONCLUSION, HE HATH *BETRAY'D* HIS FOLLOWERS, WHOSE CONDEMNATION IS PRONOUNC'D. SO FAR MY *KING* AND *MASTER;* SO MUCH MY *OFFICE.*

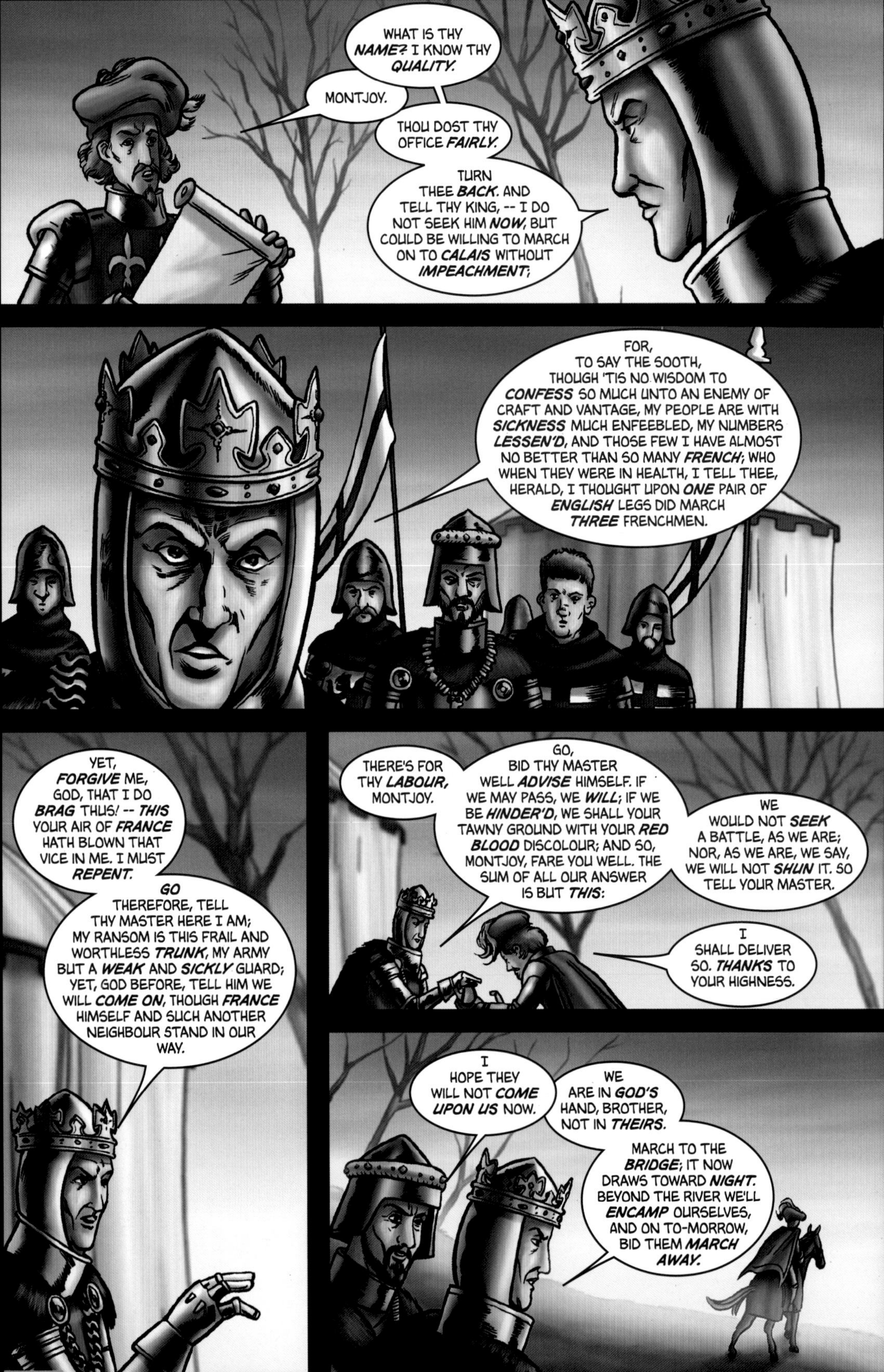
WHAT IS THY NAME? I KNOW THY QUALITY.
MONTJOY.
THOU DOST THY OFFICE FAIRLY.
TURN THEE BACK. AND TELL THY KING, -- I DO NOT SEEK HIM NOW, BUT COULD BE WILLING TO MARCH ON TO CALAIS WITHOUT IMPEACHMENT;
FOR, TO SAY THE SOOTH, THOUGH 'TIS NO WISDOM TO CONFESS SO MUCH UNTO AN ENEMY OF CRAFT AND VANTAGE, MY PEOPLE ARE WITH SICKNESS MUCH ENFEEBLED, MY NUMBERS LESSEN'D, AND THOSE FEW I HAVE ALMOST NO BETTER THAN SO MANY FRENCH; WHO WHEN THEY WERE IN HEALTH, I TELL THEE, HERALD, I THOUGHT UPON ONE PAIR OF ENGLISH LEGS DID MARCH THREE FRENCHMEN.
YET, FORGIVE ME, GOD, THAT I DO BRAG THUS! -- THIS YOUR AIR OF FRANCE HATH BLOWN THAT VICE IN ME. I MUST REPENT.
GO THEREFORE, TELL THY MASTER HERE I AM; MY RANSOM IS THIS FRAIL AND WORTHLESS TRUNK, MY ARMY BUT A WEAK AND SICKLY GUARD; YET, GOD BEFORE, TELL HIM WE WILL COME ON, THOUGH FRANCE HIMSELF AND SUCH ANOTHER NEIGHBOUR STAND IN OUR WAY.
THERE'S FOR THY LABOUR, MONTJOY.
GO, BID THY MASTER WELL ADVISE HIMSELF. IF WE MAY PASS, WE WILL; IF WE BE HINDER'D, WE SHALL YOUR TAWNY GROUND WITH YOUR RED BLOOD DISCOLOUR; AND SO, MONTJOY, FARE YOU WELL. THE SUM OF ALL OUR ANSWER IS BUT THIS:
WE WOULD NOT SEEK A BATTLE, AS WE ARE; NOR, AS WE ARE, WE SAY, WE WILL NOT SHUN IT. SO TELL YOUR MASTER.
I SHALL DELIVER SO. THANKS TO YOUR HIGHNESS.
I HOPE THEY WILL NOT COME UPON US NOW.
WE ARE IN GOD'S HAND, BROTHER, NOT IN THEIRS.
MARCH TO THE BRIDGE; IT NOW DRAWS TOWARD NIGHT. BEYOND THE RIVER WE'LL ENCAMP OURSELVES, AND ON TO-MORROW, BID THEM MARCH AWAY.

66

71

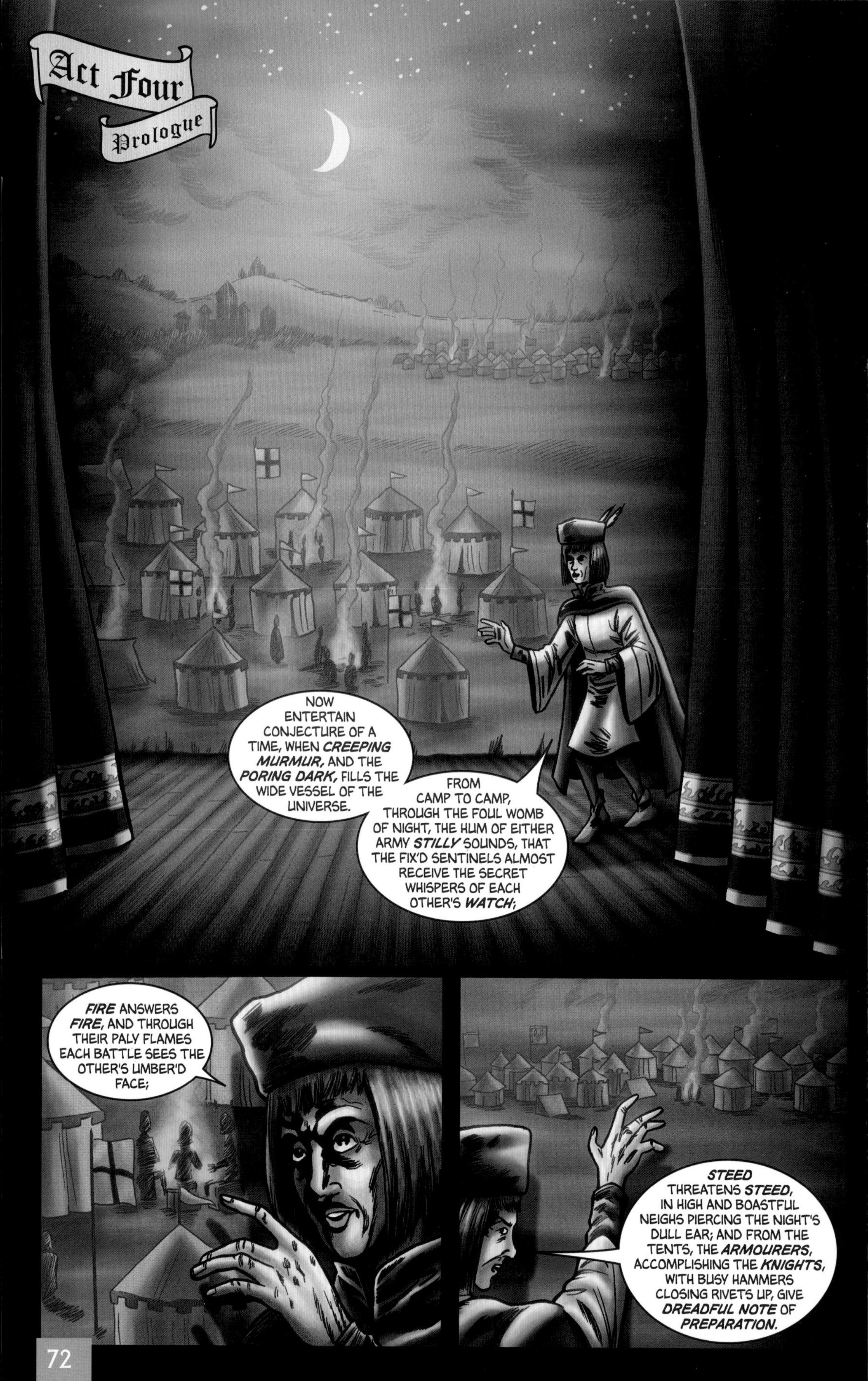
Act Four
Prologue
NOW ENTERTAIN CONJECTURE OF A TIME, WHEN CREEPING MURMUR, AND THE PORING DARK, FILLS THE WIDE VESSEL OF THE UNIVERSE.
FROM CAMP TO CAMP, THROUGH THE FOUL WOMB OF NIGHT, THE HUM OF EITHER ARMY STILLY SOUNDS, THAT THE FIX'D SENTINELS ALMOST RECEIVE THE SECRET WHISPERS OF EACH OTHER'S WATCH;
FIRE ANSWERS FIRE, AND THROUGH THEIR PALY FLAMES EACH BATTLE SEES THE OTHER'S UMBER'D FACE;
STEED THREATENS STEED, IN HIGH AND BOASTFUL NEIGHS PIERCING THE NIGHT'S DULL EAR; AND FROM THE TENTS, THE ARMOURERS, ACCOMPLISHING THE KNIGHTS, WITH BUSY HAMMERS CLOSING RIVETS UP, GIVE DREADFUL NOTE OF PREPARATION.

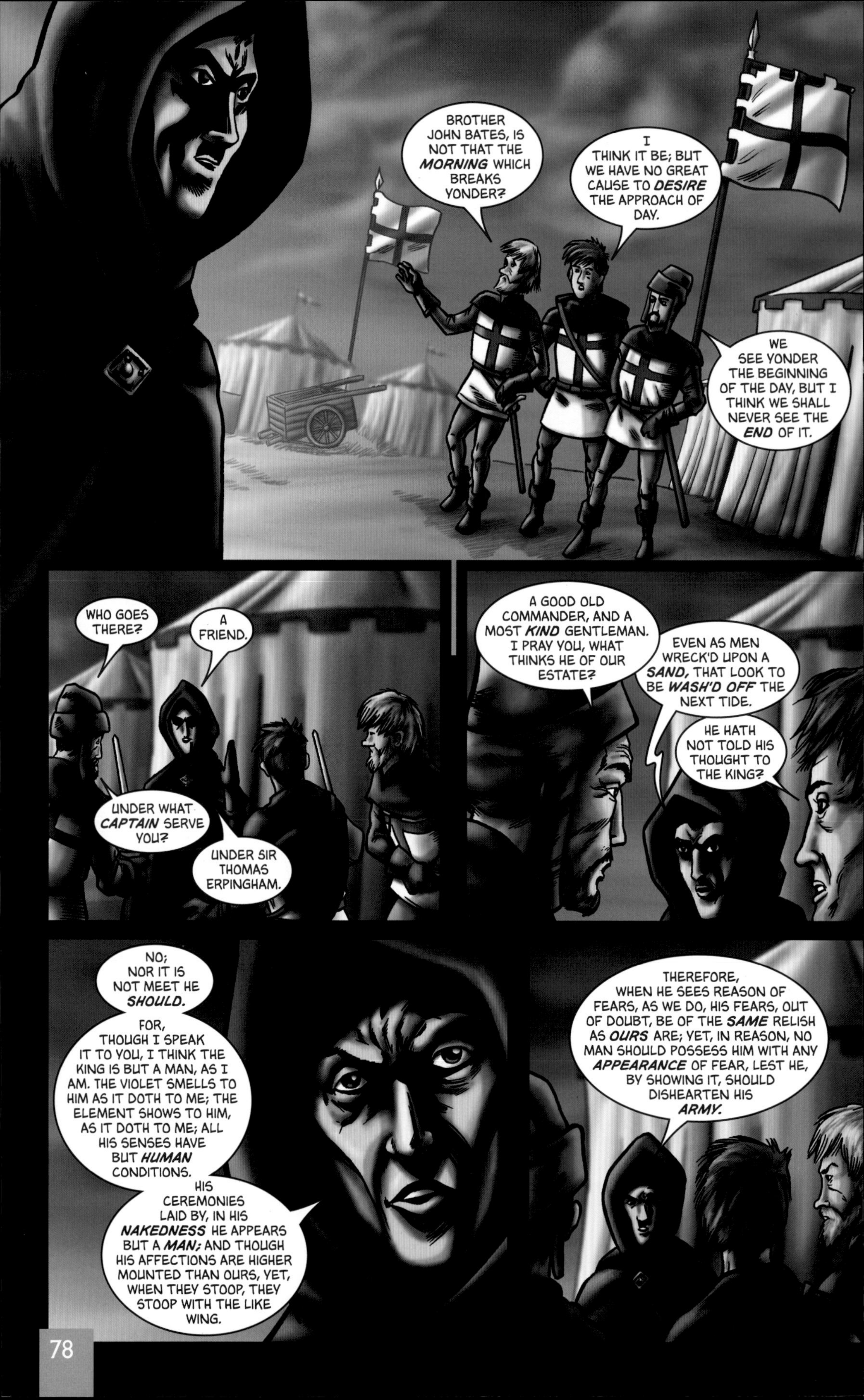
BROTHER JOHN BATES, IS NOT THAT THE MORNING WHICH BREAKS YONDER?
I THINK IT BE; BUT WE HAVE NO GREAT CAUSE TO DESIRE THE APPROACH OF DAY.
WE SEE YONDER THE BEGINNING OF THE DAY, BUT I THINK WE SHALL NEVER SEE THE END OF IT.
WHO GOES THERE?
A FRIEND.
UNDER WHAT CAPTAIN SERVE YOU?
UNDER SIR THOMAS ERPINGHAM.
A GOOD OLD COMMANDER, AND A MOST KIND GENTLEMAN. I PRAY YOU, WHAT THINKS HE OF OUR ESTATE?
EVEN AS MEN WRECK'D UPON A SAND, THAT LOOK TO BE WASH'D OFF THE NEXT TIDE.
HE HATH NOT TOLD HIS THOUGHT TO THE KING?
NO; NOR IT IS NOT MEET HE SHOULD.
FOR, THOUGH I SPEAK IT TO YOU, I THINK THE KING IS BUT A MAN, AS I AM. THE VIOLET SMELLS TO HIM AS IT DOTH TO ME; THE ELEMENT SHOWS TO HIM, AS IT DOTH TO ME; ALL HIS SENSES HAVE BUT HUMAN CONDITIONS.
HIS CEREMONIES LAID BY, IN HIS NAKEDNESS HE APPEARS BUT A MAN; AND THOUGH HIS AFFECTIONS ARE HIGHER MOUNTED THAN OURS, YET, WHEN THEY STOOP, THEY STOOP WITH THE LIKE WING.
THEREFORE, WHEN HE SEES REASON OF FEARS, AS WE DO, HIS FEARS, OUT OF DOUBT, BE OF THE SAME RELISH AS OURS ARE; YET, IN REASON, NO MAN SHOULD POSSESS HIM WITH ANY APPEARANCE OF FEAR, LEST HE, BY SHOWING IT, SHOULD DISHEARTEN HIS ARMY.

79

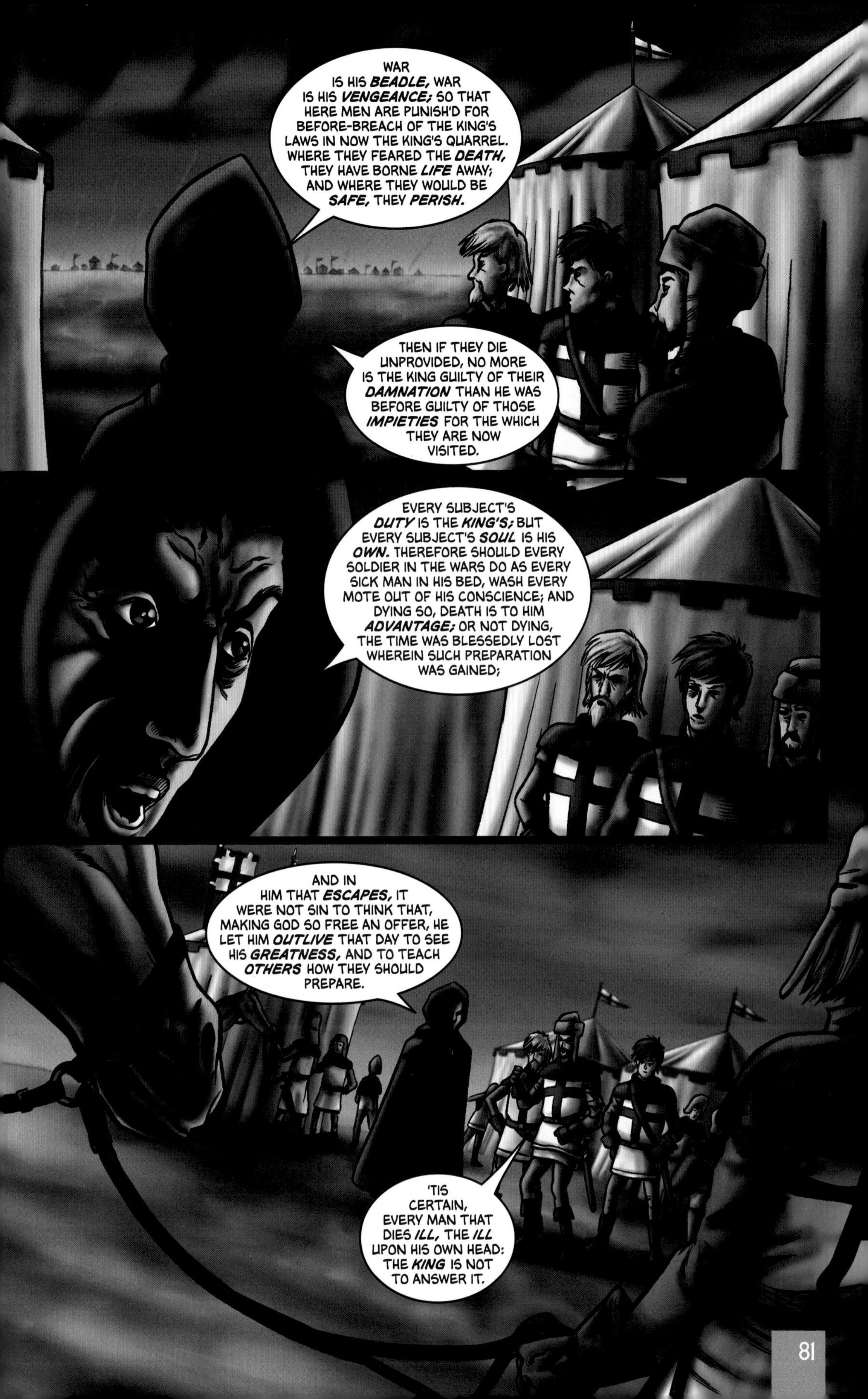
WAR IS HIS BEADLE, WAR IS HIS VENGEANCE; SO THAT HERE MEN ARE PUNISH'D FOR BEFORE-BREACH OF THE KING'S LAWS IN NOW THE KING'S QUARREL. WHERE THEY FEARED THE DEATH, THEY HAVE BORNE LIFE AWAY; AND WHERE THEY WOULD BE SAFE, THEY PERISH.
THEN IF THEY DIE UNPROVIDED, NO MORE IS THE KING GUILTY OF THEIR DAMNATION THAN HE WAS BEFORE GUILTY OF THOSE IMPIETIES FOR THE WHICH THEY ARE NOW VISITED.
EVERY SUBJECT'S DUTY IS THE KING'S; BUT EVERY SUBJECT'S SOUL IS HIS OWN. THEREFORE SHOULD EVERY SOLDIER IN THE WARS DO AS EVERY SICK MAN IN HIS BED, WASH EVERY MOTE OUT OF HIS CONSCIENCE; AND DYING SO, DEATH IS TO HIM ADVANTAGE; OR NOT DYING, THE TIME WAS BLESSEDLY LOST WHEREIN SUCH PREPARATION WAS GAINED;
AND IN HIM THAT ESCAPES, IT WERE NOT SIN TO THINK THAT, MAKING GOD SO FREE AN OFFER, HE LET HIM OUTLIVE THAT DAY TO SEE HIS GREATNESS, AND TO TEACH OTHERS HOW THEY SHOULD PREPARE.
'TIS CERTAIN, EVERY MAN THAT DIES ILL, THE ILL UPON HIS OWN HEAD: THE KING IS NOT TO ANSWER IT.

83

89

THE ENGLISH CAMP, AGINCOURT - OCTOBER 25TH 1415. THE MORNING OF THE BATTLE...

WHERE IS THE *KING?*

THE KING *HIMSELF* IS RODE TO VIEW THEIR BATTLE.

OF FIGHTING MEN THEY HAVE FULL *THREE-SCORE THOUSAND.*

THERE'S FIVE TO ONE; BESIDES, THEY ALL ARE *FRESH.*

GOD'S ARM STRIKE WITH US! 'TIS A *FEARFUL* ODDS.

GOD BE WI' YOU, PRINCES ALL; I'LL TO MY CHARGE. IF WE *NO MORE* MEET, TILL WE MEET IN *HEAVEN,* THEN, JOYFULLY,

MY NOBLE *LORD OF BEDFORD,* -- MY DEAR *LORD GLOUCESTER,* -- AND MY GOOD *LORD EXETER,* -- AND MY KIND KINSMAN, -- *WARRIORS ALL, ADIEU!*

FAREWELL, GOOD SALISBURY, AND *GOOD LUCK* GO WITH THEE!

FAREWELL, KIND LORD. FIGHT *VALIANTLY* TO-DAY! AND YET I DO THEE WRONG TO MIND THEE OF IT, FOR THOU ART *FRAM'D* OF THE FIRM TRUTH OF VALOUR.

HE IS AS FULL OF *VALOUR* AS OF *KINDNESS;* PRINCELY IN *BOTH.*

O! THAT WE NOW HAD HERE BUT ONE *TEN THOUSAND* OF THOSE MEN IN ENGLAND, THAT DO NO WORK TO-DAY!

WHAT'S HE THAT WISHES SO? MY COUSIN WESTMORELAND? -- NO, MY FAIR COUSIN. IF WE ARE MARK'D TO *DIE,* WE ARE ENOW TO DO OUR COUNTRY LOSS; AND IF TO *LIVE,* THE FEWER MEN, THE GREATER SHARE OF *HONOUR.*

GOD'S WILL! I PRAY THEE, WISH NOT ONE MAN MORE.

GOOD ARGUMENT, I HOPE, WE WILL NOT *FLY* -- AND TIME HATH WORN US INTO *SLOVENRY*; BUT, BY THE MASS, OUR *HEARTS* ARE IN THE TRIM;

AND MY POOR SOLDIERS TELL ME, YET ERE NIGHT THEY'LL BE IN *FRESHER* ROBES, OR THEY WILL PLUCK THE GAY NEW COATS O'ER THE FRENCH SOLDIERS' *HEADS* AND TURN THEM OUT OF SERVICE. IF THEY DO THIS -- AS, IF GOD PLEASE, THEY SHALL, -- MY *RANSOM* THEN WILL *SOON* BE LEVIED.

HERALD, SAVE THOU THY *LABOUR.* COME THOU *NO MORE* FOR RANSOM, GENTLE HERALD.

THEY SHALL HAVE *NONE,* I SWEAR, BUT THESE MY *JOINTS;* WHICH IF THEY HAVE AS I WILL LEAVE 'EM THEM, SHALL YIELD THEM *LITTLE,* TELL THE CONSTABLE.

I *SHALL,* KING HARRY. AND SO FARE THEE WELL; THOU NEVER SHALT HEAR HERALD ANY MORE.

I FEAR, THOU'LT ONCE MORE COME *AGAIN* FOR RANSOM.

MY LORD, MOST HUMBLY ON MY KNEE I BEG THE *LEADING* OF THE *VAWARD.*

AND HOW THOU PLEASEST, GOD, DISPOSE THE DAY!

TAKE IT, BRAVE YORK. *NOW, SOLDIERS, MARCH AWAY;*

95

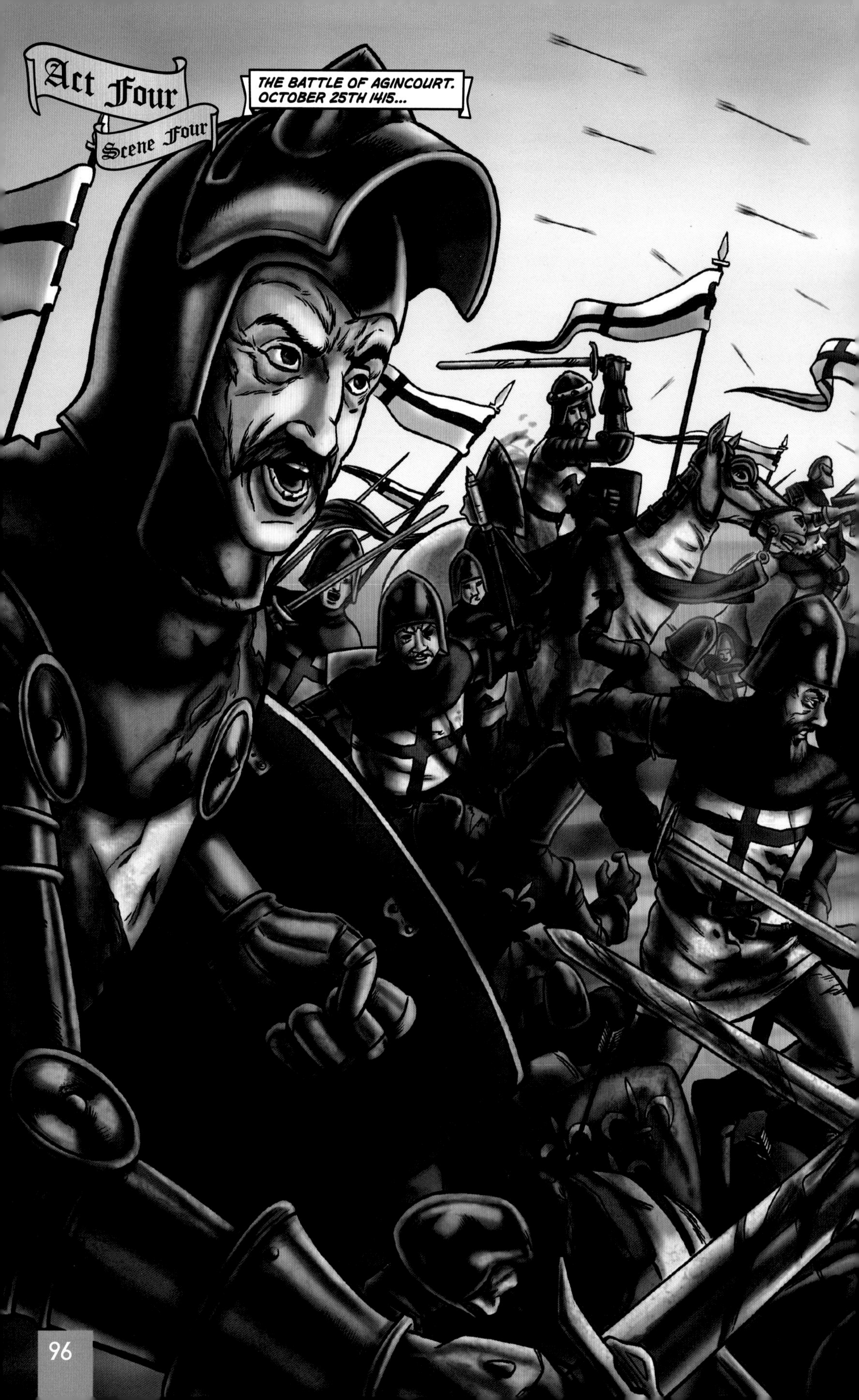
Act Four
Scene Four
THE BATTLE OF AGINCOURT. OCTOBER 25TH 1415...

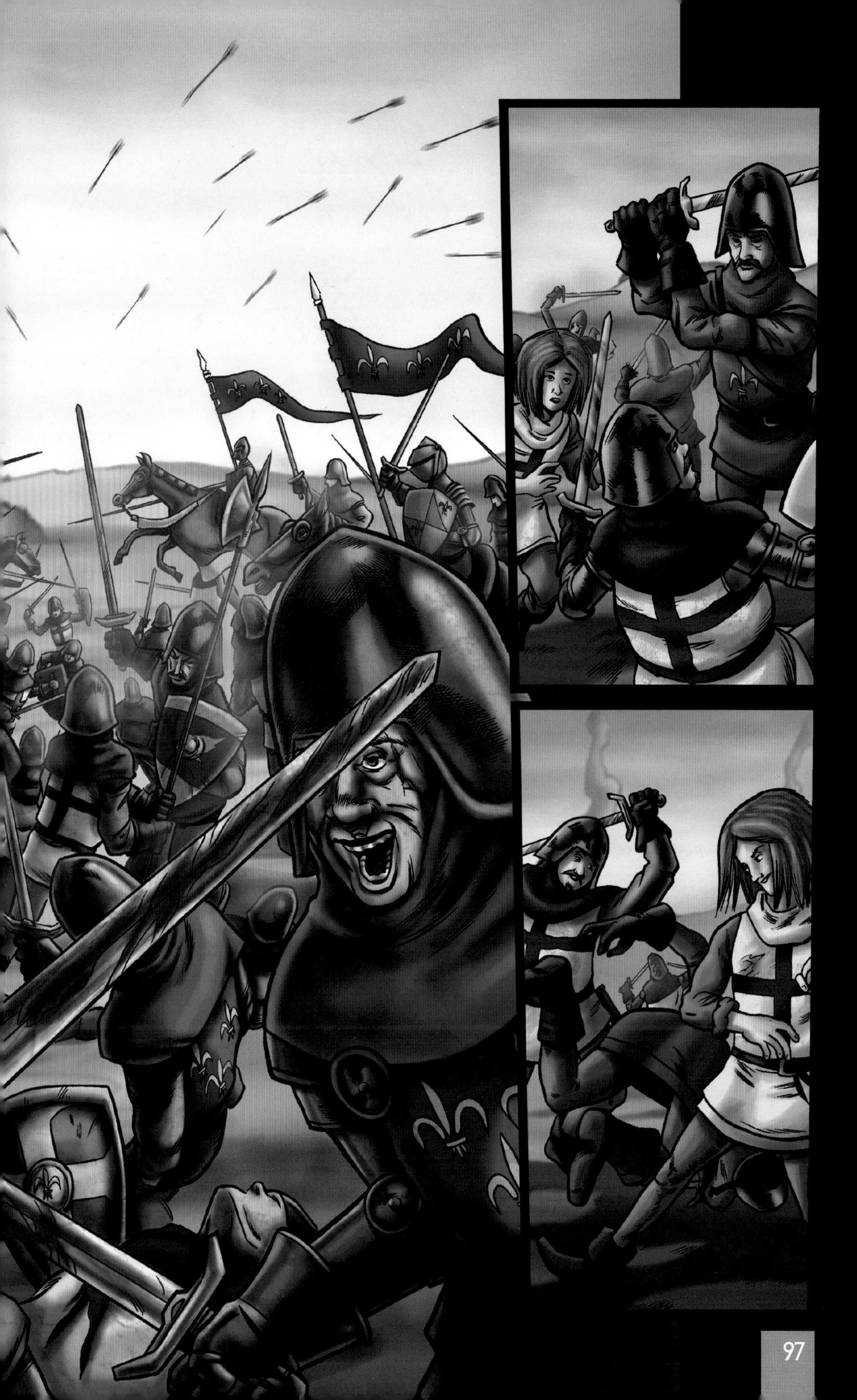

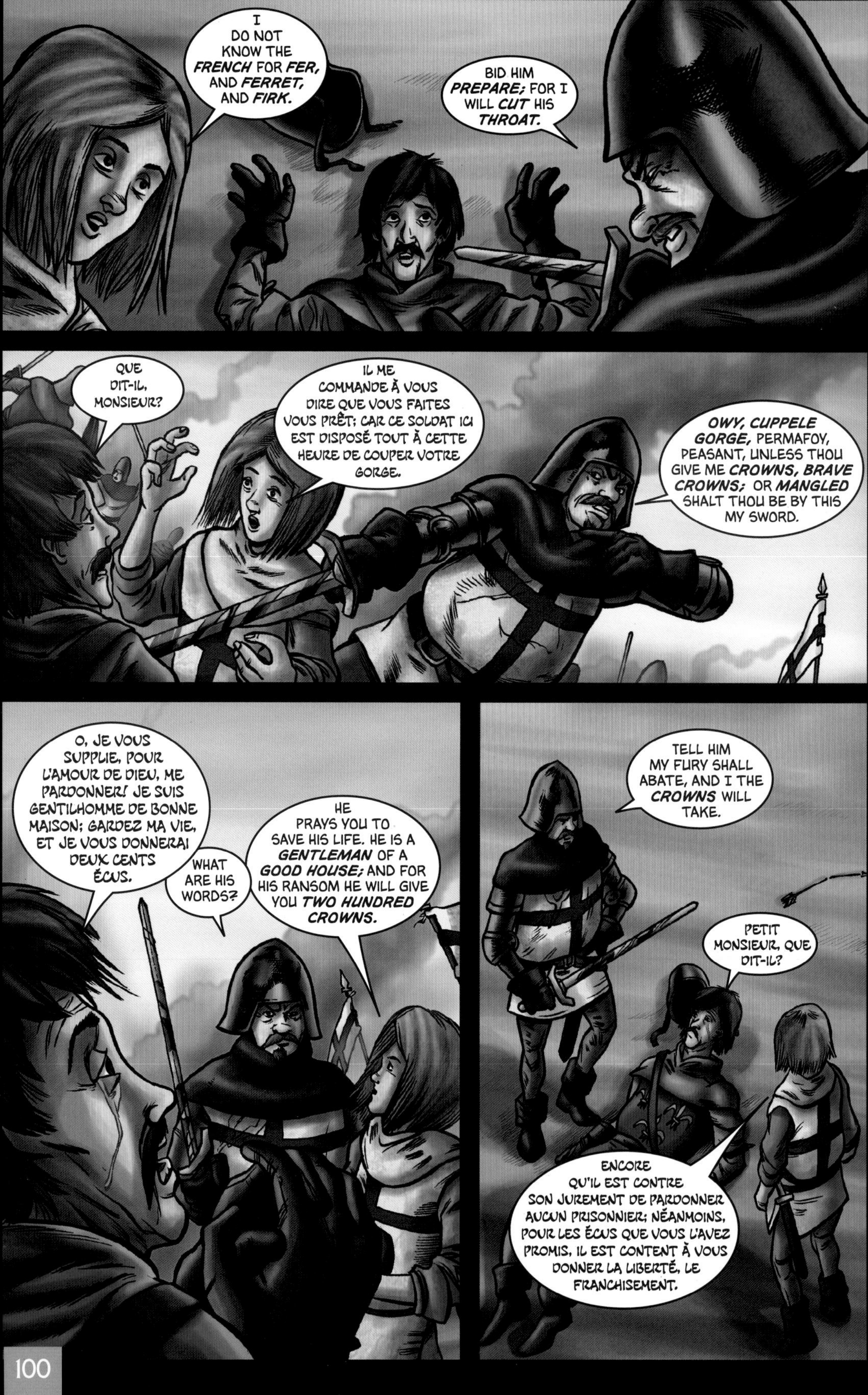
I DO NOT KNOW THE FRENCH FOR FER, AND FERRET, AND FIRK.
BID HIM PREPARE; FOR I WILL CUT HIS THROAT.
QUE DIT-IL, MONSIEUR?
IL ME COMMANDE À VOUS DIRE QUE VOUS FAITES VOUS PRÊT; CAR CE SOLDAT ICI EST DISPOSÉ TOUT À CETTE HEURE DE COUPER VOTRE GORGE.
OWY, CUPPELE GORGE, PERMAFOY, PEASANT, UNLESS THOU GIVE ME CROWNS, BRAVE CROWNS; OR MANGLED SHALT THOU BE BY THIS MY SWORD.
O, JE VOUS SUPPLIE, POUR L'AMOUR DE DIEU, ME PARDONNER! JE SUIS GENTILHOMME DE BONNE MAISON; GARDEZ MA VIE, ET JE VOUS DONNERAI DEUX CENTS ÉCUS.
WHAT ARE HIS WORDS?
HE PRAYS YOU TO SAVE HIS LIFE. HE IS A GENTLEMAN OF A GOOD HOUSE; AND FOR HIS RANSOM HE WILL GIVE YOU TWO HUNDRED CROWNS.
TELL HIM MY FURY SHALL ABATE, AND I THE CROWNS WILL TAKE.
PETIT MONSIEUR, QUE DIT-IL?
ENCORE QU'IL EST CONTRE SON JUREMENT DE PARDONNER AUCUN PRISONNIER; NÉANMOINS, POUR LES ÉCUS QUE VOUS L'AVEZ PROMIS, IL EST CONTENT À VOUS DONNER LA LIBERTÉ, LE FRANCHISEMENT.

ON THE FRENCH SIDE OF THE BATTLEFIELD. THE FRENCH ARE LOSING...

DIABLE!

SEIGNEUR! LE JOUR EST PERDU, TOUT EST PERDU!

MORT DE MA VIE! ALL IS CONFOUNDED, ALL! REPROACH AND EVERLASTING SHAME SITS MOCKING IN OUR PLUMES. O MÉCHANTE FORTUNE!

TAN-TARA!

DO NOT RUN AWAY.

WHY, ALL OUR RANKS ARE BROKE.

PERDURABLE SHAME! -- LET'S STAB OURSELVES, BE THESE THE WRETCHES THAT WE PLAY'D AT DICE FOR?

IS THIS THE KING WE SENT TO FOR HIS RANSOM?

SHAME AND ETERNAL SHAME, NOTHING BUT SHAME! LET'S DIE IN HONOUR! -- ONCE MORE BACK AGAIN! AND HE THAT WILL NOT FOLLOW BOURBON NOW, LET HIM GO HENCE, AND WITH HIS CAP IN HAND, LIKE A BASE PANDAR, HOLD THE CHAMBER DOOR WHILST BY A SLAVE, NO GENTLER THAN MY DOG, HIS FAIREST DAUGHTER IS CONTAMINATED.

DISORDER, THAT HATH SPOIL'D US, FRIEND US NOW! LET US, ON HEAPS, GO OFFER UP OUR LIVES.

WE ARE ENOUGH, YET LIVING IN THE FIELD, TO SMOTHER UP THE ENGLISH IN OUR THRONGS, IF ANY ORDER MIGHT BE THOUGHT UPON.

THE DEVIL TAKE ORDER NOW! I'LL TO THE THRONG. LET LIFE BE SHORT, ELSE SHAME WILL BE TOO LONG.

I THINK IT IS IN *MACEDON* WHERE ALEXANDER IS PORN. I *TELL* YOU, CAPTAIN, IF YOU LOOK IN THE MAPS OF THE 'ORLD, I WARRANT, YOU SHALL FIND, IN THE COMPARISONS BETWEEN *MACEDON* AND *MONMOUTH,* THAT THE SITUATIONS, LOOK YOU, IS BOTH *ALIKE.*

THERE IS A *RIVER* IN MACEDON; AND THERE IS ALSO MOREOVER A RIVER AT *MONMOUTH;* IT IS CALL'D *WYE* AT MONMOUTH;

BUT IT IS OUT OF MY PRAINS WHAT IS THE NAME OF THE *OTHER* RIVER; BUT 'TIS ALL ONE, 'TIS ALIKE AS MY FINGERS IS TO MY FINGERS, AND THERE IS *SALMONS* IN BOTH. IF YOU MARK *ALEXANDER'S* LIFE WELL, *HARRY OF MONMOUTH'S* LIFE IS COME *AFTER* IT INDIFFERENT WELL; FOR THERE IS FIGURES IN *ALL* THINGS.

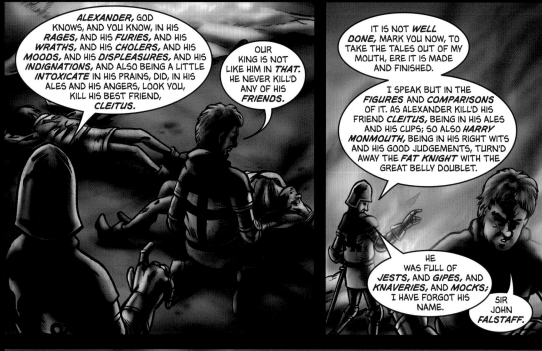

ALEXANDER, GOD KNOWS, AND YOU KNOW, IN HIS *RAGES,* AND HIS *FURIES,* AND HIS *WRATHS,* AND HIS *CHOLERS,* AND HIS *MOODS,* AND HIS *DISPLEASURES,* AND HIS *INDIGNATIONS,* AND ALSO BEING A LITTLE *INTOXICATE* IN HIS PRAINS, DID, IN HIS ALES AND HIS ANGERS, LOOK YOU, KILL HIS BEST FRIEND, *CLEITUS.*

OUR KING IS NOT LIKE HIM IN *THAT.* HE NEVER KILL'D ANY OF HIS *FRIENDS.*

IT IS NOT *WELL DONE,* MARK YOU NOW, TO TAKE THE TALES OUT OF MY MOUTH, ERE IT IS MADE AND FINISHED.

I SPEAK BUT IN THE *FIGURES* AND *COMPARISONS* OF IT. AS ALEXANDER KILL'D HIS FRIEND *CLEITUS,* BEING IN HIS ALES AND HIS CUPS; SO ALSO *HARRY MONMOUTH,* BEING IN HIS RIGHT WITS AND HIS GOOD JUDGEMENTS, TURN'D AWAY THE *FAT KNIGHT* WITH THE GREAT BELLY DOUBLET.

HE WAS FULL OF *JESTS,* AND *GIPES,* AND *KNAVERIES,* AND *MOCKS;* I HAVE FORGOT HIS NAME.

SIR JOHN *FALSTAFF.*

THAT IS HE. I'LL *TELL* YOU THERE IS *GOOD MEN* PORN AT MONMOUTH.

HERE COMES *HIS* MAJESTY.

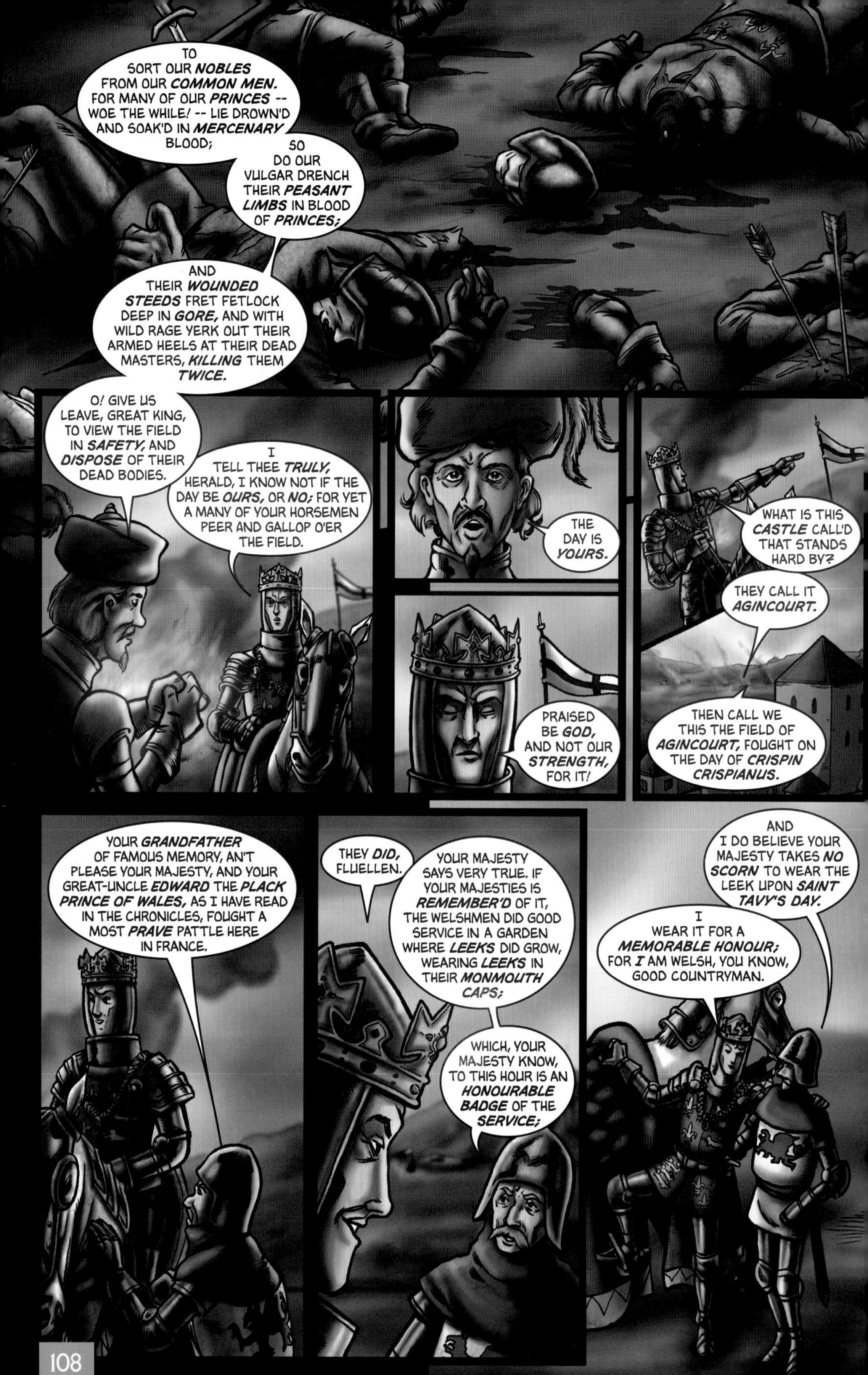

TO SORT OUR *NOBLES* FROM OUR *COMMON MEN.* FOR MANY OF OUR *PRINCES* -- WOE THE WHILE! -- LIE DROWN'D AND SOAK'D IN *MERCENARY* BLOOD;
SO DO OUR VULGAR DRENCH THEIR *PEASANT LIMBS* IN BLOOD OF *PRINCES;*
AND THEIR *WOUNDED STEEDS* FRET FETLOCK DEEP IN *GORE,* AND WITH WILD RAGE YERK OUT THEIR ARMED HEELS AT THEIR DEAD MASTERS, *KILLING* THEM *TWICE.*
O! GIVE US LEAVE, GREAT KING, TO VIEW THE FIELD IN *SAFETY,* AND *DISPOSE* OF THEIR DEAD BODIES.
I TELL THEE *TRULY,* HERALD, I KNOW NOT IF THE DAY BE *OURS,* OR *NO;* FOR YET A MANY OF YOUR HORSEMEN PEER AND GALLOP O'ER THE FIELD.
THE DAY IS *YOURS.*
PRAISED BE *GOD,* AND NOT OUR *STRENGTH,* FOR IT!
WHAT IS THIS *CASTLE* CALL'D THAT STANDS HARD BY?
THEY CALL IT *AGINCOURT.*
THEN CALL WE THIS THE FIELD OF *AGINCOURT,* FOUGHT ON THE DAY OF *CRISPIN CRISPIANUS.*
YOUR *GRANDFATHER* OF FAMOUS MEMORY, AN'T PLEASE YOUR MAJESTY, AND YOUR GREAT-UNCLE *EDWARD* THE *PLACK PRINCE OF WALES,* AS I HAVE READ IN THE CHRONICLES, FOUGHT A MOST *PRAVE* PATTLE HERE IN FRANCE.
THEY *DID,* FLUELLEN.
YOUR MAJESTY SAYS VERY TRUE. IF YOUR MAJESTIES IS *REMEMBER'D* OF IT, THE WELSHMEN DID GOOD SERVICE IN A GARDEN WHERE *LEEKS* DID GROW, WEARING *LEEKS* IN THEIR *MONMOUTH CAPS;*
WHICH, YOUR MAJESTY KNOW, TO THIS HOUR IS AN *HONOURABLE BADGE* OF THE *SERVICE;*
AND I DO BELIEVE YOUR MAJESTY TAKES *NO SCORN* TO WEAR THE LEEK UPON *SAINT TAVY'S DAY.*
I WEAR IT FOR A *MEMORABLE HONOUR;* FOR *I* AM WELSH, YOU KNOW, GOOD COUNTRYMAN.

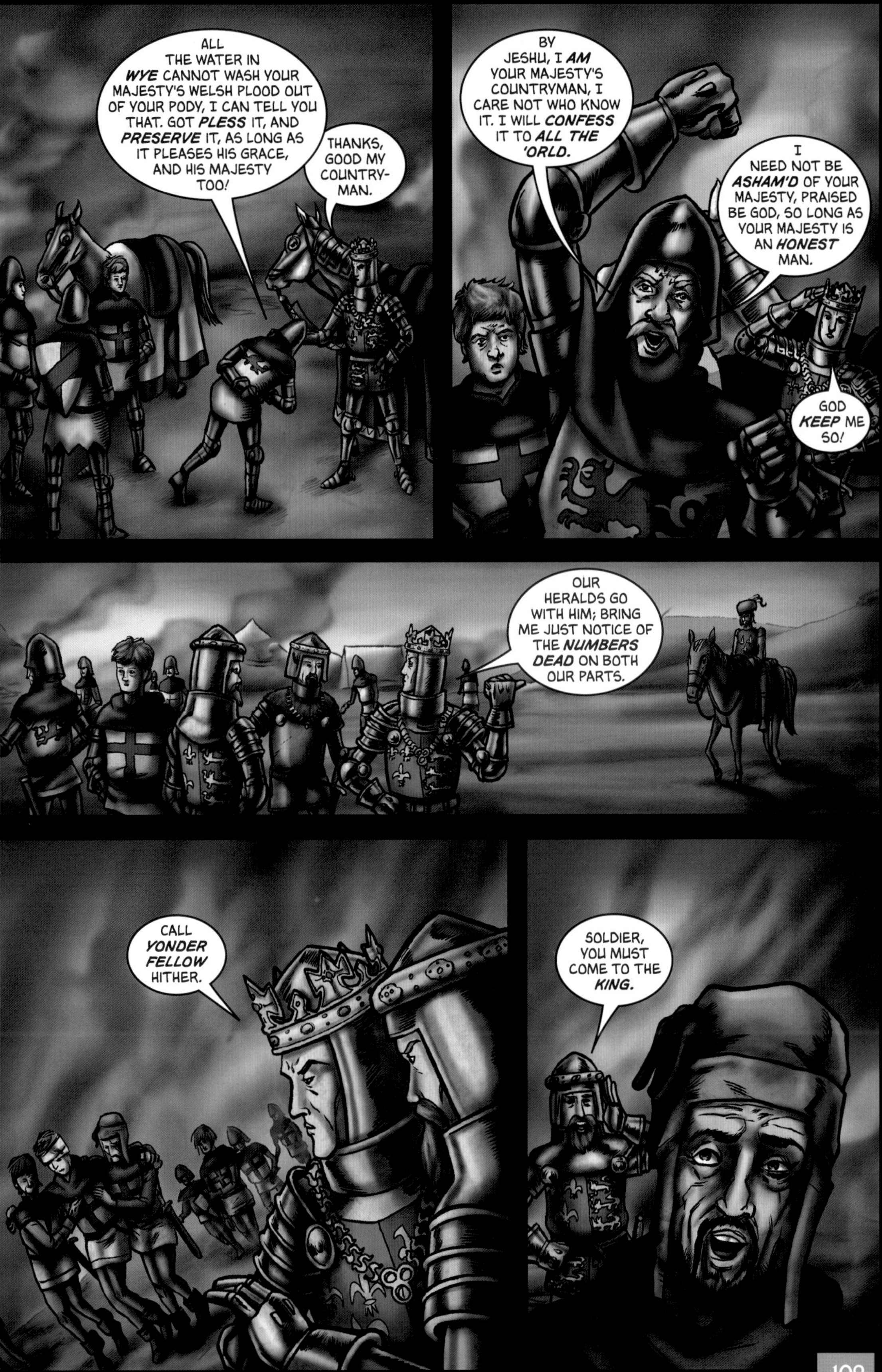
ALL THE WATER IN WYE CANNOT WASH YOUR MAJESTY'S WELSH PLOOD OUT OF YOUR PODY, I CAN TELL YOU THAT. GOT PLESS IT, AND PRESERVE IT, AS LONG AS IT PLEASES HIS GRACE, AND HIS MAJESTY TOO!
THANKS, GOOD MY COUNTRYMAN.
BY JESHU, I AM YOUR MAJESTY'S COUNTRYMAN, I CARE NOT WHO KNOW IT. I WILL CONFESS IT TO ALL THE 'ORLD.
I NEED NOT BE ASHAM'D OF YOUR MAJESTY, PRAISED BE GOD, SO LONG AS YOUR MAJESTY IS AN HONEST MAN.
GOD KEEP ME SO!
OUR HERALDS GO WITH HIM; BRING ME JUST NOTICE OF THE NUMBERS DEAD ON BOTH OUR PARTS.
CALL YONDER FELLOW HITHER.
SOLDIER, YOU MUST COME TO THE KING.

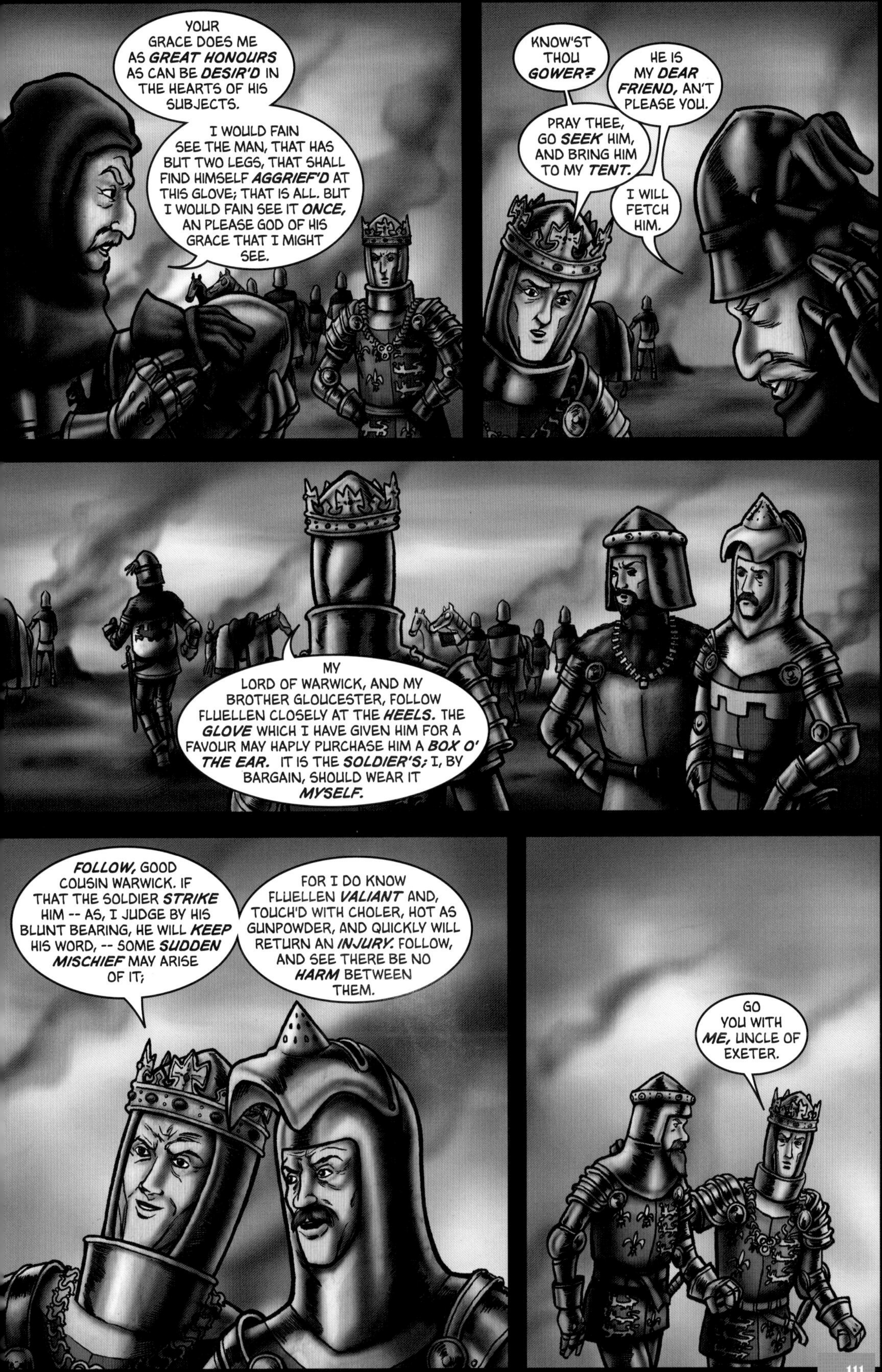
YOUR GRACE DOES ME AS GREAT HONOURS AS CAN BE DESIR'D IN THE HEARTS OF HIS SUBJECTS.
I WOULD FAIN SEE THE MAN, THAT HAS BUT TWO LEGS, THAT SHALL FIND HIMSELF AGGRIEF'D AT THIS GLOVE; THAT IS ALL. BUT I WOULD FAIN SEE IT ONCE, AN PLEASE GOD OF HIS GRACE THAT I MIGHT SEE.
KNOW'ST THOU GOWER?
HE IS MY DEAR FRIEND, AN'T PLEASE YOU.
PRAY THEE, GO SEEK HIM, AND BRING HIM TO MY TENT.
I WILL FETCH HIM.
MY LORD OF WARWICK, AND MY BROTHER GLOUCESTER, FOLLOW FLUELLEN CLOSELY AT THE HEELS. THE GLOVE WHICH I HAVE GIVEN HIM FOR A FAVOUR MAY HAPLY PURCHASE HIM A BOX O' THE EAR. IT IS THE SOLDIER'S; I, BY BARGAIN, SHOULD WEAR IT MYSELF.
FOLLOW, GOOD COUSIN WARWICK. IF THAT THE SOLDIER STRIKE HIM -- AS, I JUDGE BY HIS BLUNT BEARING, HE WILL KEEP HIS WORD, -- SOME SUDDEN MISCHIEF MAY ARISE OF IT;
FOR I DO KNOW FLUELLEN VALIANT AND, TOUCH'D WITH CHOLER, HOT AS GUNPOWDER, AND QUICKLY WILL RETURN AN INJURY. FOLLOW, AND SEE THERE BE NO HARM BETWEEN THEM.
GO YOU WITH ME, UNCLE OF EXETER.

THE ENGLISH CAMP, AGINCOURT. OUTSIDE THE REMAINS OF THE KING'S TENT...

I warrant it is to *knight* you, Captain.

GOD'S *WILL* AND HIS *PLEASURE*, CAPTAIN, I BESEECH YOU NOW, COME APACE TO THE *KING*. THERE IS MORE *GOOD* TOWARD YOU PERADVENTURE THAN IS IN YOUR KNOWLEDGE TO *DREAM* OF.

SIR, KNOW YOU THIS *GLOVE?*

KNOW THE GLOVE? I KNOW THE GLOVE IS A *GLOVE*.

I KNOW *THIS;*

AND THUS I *CHALLENGE* IT.

SMAAAACK!!!

'SBLOOD! AN ARRANT *TRAITOR* AS ANY'S IN THE UNIVERSAL 'ORLD, OR IN *FRANCE*, OR IN *ENGLAND!*

HOW NOW, SIR! YOU VILLAIN!

DO YOU THINK I'LL BE *FOR-SWORN?*

STAND *AWAY*, CAPTAIN GOWER. I WILL GIVE TREASON HIS PAYMENT INTO *PLOWS*, I WARRANT YOU.

HOW CANST THOU MAKE ME *SATISFACTION?*

ALL OFFENCES, MY LORD, COME FROM THE *HEART.* NEVER CAME ANY FROM MINE, THAT MIGHT *OFFEND* YOUR MAJESTY.

IT WAS *OURSELF* THOU DIDST *ABUSE.*

YOUR MAJESTY CAME NOT *LIKE* YOURSELF. YOU APPEAR'D TO ME BUT AS A *COMMON MAN;* WITNESS THE NIGHT, YOUR GARMENTS, YOUR LOWLINESS; AND WHAT YOUR HIGHNESS *SUFFER'D* UNDER THAT SHAPE, I BESEECH YOU TAKE IT FOR YOUR *OWN* FAULT AND NOT *MINE;*

FOR HAD YOU BEEN AS I *TOOK* YOU FOR, I MADE *NO* OFFENCE; THEREFORE, I BESEECH YOUR HIGHNESS, *PARDON* ME.

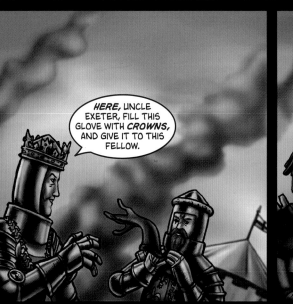

HERE, UNCLE EXETER, FILL THIS GLOVE WITH *CROWNS,* AND GIVE IT TO THIS FELLOW.

KEEP IT, FELLOW; AND WEAR IT FOR AN HONOUR IN THY CAP, TILL I DO *CHALLENGE* IT. -- GIVE HIM THE CROWNS; -- AND, CAPTAIN, YOU MUST NEEDS BE *FRIENDS* WITH HIM.

BY THIS DAY AND THIS LIGHT, THE FELLOW HAS *METTLE* ENOUGH IN HIS BELLY.

HOLD, THERE IS *TWELVE PENCE* FOR YOU; AND I PRAY YOU TO SERVE GOD, AND KEEP YOU OUT OF PRAWLS, AND PRABBLES, AND QUARRELS, AND DISSENSIONS; AND, I WARRANT YOU, IT IS THE *BETTER* FOR YOU.

I WILL *NONE* OF *YOUR* MONEY.

IT IS WITH A GOOD WILL; I CAN TELL YOU, IT WILL *SERVE* YOU TO MEND YOUR *SHOES.* COME, WHEREFORE SHOULD YOU BE SO *PASHFUL?* YOUR SHOES IS NOT SO GOOD. 'TIS A *GOOD* SILLING, I WARRANT YOU, OR I WILL *CHANGE* IT.

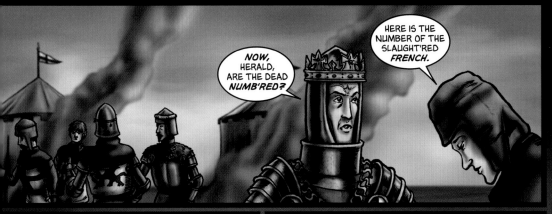

NOW, ARE THE DEAD NUMB'RED?

HERE IS THE NUMBER OF THE SLAUGHT'RED *FRENCH.*

WHAT PRISONERS OF *GOOD SORT* ARE TAKEN, UNCLE?

CHARLES DUKE OF ORLEANS, NEPHEW TO THE KING; *JOHN DUKE OF BOURBON,* AND *LORD BOUCIQUALT:* OF OTHER LORDS AND BARONS, KNIGHTS AND SQUIRES, FULL *FIFTEEN HUNDRED,* BESIDES COMMON MEN.

THIS NOTE DOTH TELL ME OF *TEN THOUSAND FRENCH,* THAT IN THE FIELD LIE SLAIN; OF PRINCES, IN THIS NUMBER, AND NOBLES BEARING BANNERS, THERE LIE DEAD *ONE HUNDRED TWENTY-SIX;*

ADDED TO THESE, OF KNIGHTS, ESQUIRES, AND GALLANT GENTLEMEN, *EIGHT THOUSAND AND FOUR HUNDRED;* OF THE WHICH, *FIVE HUNDRED* WERE BUT *YESTERDAY* DUBB'D KNIGHTS;

JOHN *DUKE OF ALENÇON, ANTHONY DUKE OF BRABANT,* THE BROTHER TO THE DUKE OF BURGUNDY, AND *EDWARD DUKE OF BAR;* OF LUSTY EARLS, GRANDPRÉ AND ROUSSI, FAUCONBERG AND FOIX, BEAUMONT AND MARLE, VAUDEMONT AND LESTRALE. HERE WAS A *ROYAL* FELLOWSHIP OF DEATH!

SO THAT, IN THESE TEN THOUSAND THEY HAVE LOST, THERE ARE BUT SIXTEEN HUNDRED MERCENARIES; THE REST ARE *PRINCES, BARONS, LORDS, KNIGHTS, SQUIRES,* AND GENTLEMEN OF *BLOOD* AND *QUALITY.*

THE NAMES OF THOSE THEIR NOBLES THAT LIE DEAD: *CHARLES DELABRETH,* HIGH CONSTABLE OF FRANCE; *JACQUES OF CHATILLON,* ADMIRAL OF FRANCE; THE MASTER OF THE CROSS-BOWS, LORD RAMBURES; GREAT MASTER OF FRANCE, THE BRAVE *SIR GUICHARD DAUPHIN,*

WHERE IS THE NUMBER OF OUR *ENGLISH* DEAD?

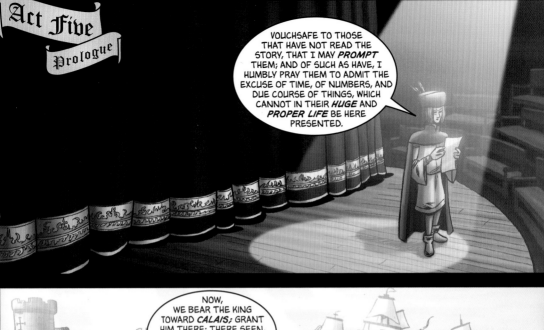

VOUCHSAFE TO THOSE THAT HAVE NOT READ THE STORY, THAT I MAY *PROMPT* THEM; AND OF SUCH AS HAVE, I HUMBLY PRAY THEM TO ADMIT THE EXCUSE OF TIME, OF NUMBERS, AND DUE COURSE OF THINGS, WHICH CANNOT IN THEIR *HUGE* AND *PROPER LIFE* BE HERE PRESENTED.

NOW, WE BEAR THE KING TOWARD *CALAIS*; GRANT HIM THERE; THERE SEEN, HEAVE HIM AWAY UPON YOUR WINGED THOUGHTS ATHWART THE SEA.

BEHOLD, THE ENGLISH BEACH PALES IN THE *FLOOD* WITH *MEN*, WITH *WIVES* AND *BOYS*, WHOSE SHOUTS AND CLAPS *OUT-VOICE* THE DEEP-MOUTH'D *SEA*, WHICH LIKE A *MIGHTY WHIFFLER* 'FORE THE KING SEEMS TO PREPARE HIS WAY.

SO, LET HIM LAND, AND SOLEMNLY SEE HIM SET ON TO *LONDON*. SO SWIFT A PACE HATH THOUGHT, THAT EVEN NOW YOU MAY IMAGINE HIM UPON *BLACKHEATH*; WHERE THAT HIS *LORDS* DESIRE HIM TO HAVE BORNE HIS BRUISED HELMET, AND HIS BENDED SWORD, *BEFORE* HIM, THROUGH THE *CITY*. HE *FORBIDS* IT, BEING *FREE* FROM *VAINNESS* AND SELF-GLORIOUS *PRIDE*; GIVING FULL TROPHY, SIGNAL, AND OSTENT, QUITE FROM HIMSELF, TO *GOD*.

BUT NOW BEHOLD, IN THE QUICK FORGE AND WORKING-HOUSE OF THOUGHT, HOW *LONDON* DOTH *POUR OUT* HER CITIZENS. THE *MAYOR* AND ALL HIS BRETHREN IN BEST SORT, LIKE TO THE *SENATORS* OF THE ANTIQUE ROME, WITH THE *PLEBEIANS* SWARMING AT THEIR HEELS, GO FORTH AND FETCH THEIR *CONQUERING CAESAR* IN;

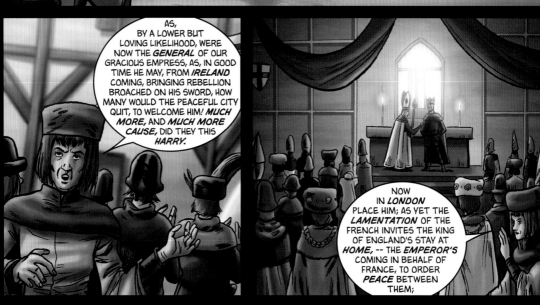

AS, BY A LOWER BUT LOVING LIKELIHOOD, WERE NOW THE *GENERAL* OF OUR GRACIOUS EMPRESS, AS, IN GOOD TIME HE MAY, FROM *IRELAND* COMING, BRINGING REBELLION BROACHED ON HIS SWORD, HOW MANY WOULD THE PEACEFUL CITY QUIT, TO WELCOME HIM! *MUCH MORE*, AND *MUCH MORE CAUSE*, DID THEY THIS *HARRY*.

NOW IN *LONDON* PLACE HIM; AS YET THE *LAMENTATION* OF THE FRENCH INVITES THE KING OF ENGLAND'S STAY AT *HOME*, -- THE *EMPEROR'S* COMING IN BEHALF OF FRANCE, TO ORDER *PEACE* BETWEEN THEM;

AND OMIT ALL THE OCCURRENCES, WHATEVER CHANC'D, TILL HARRY'S *BACK-RETURN* AGAIN TO *FRANCE.* THERE MUST WE BRING HIM; AND MYSELF HAVE PLAY'D THE INTERIM, BY REMEMBERING YOU 'TIS PAST. THEN BROOK ABRIDGMENT, AND YOUR EYES ADVANCE AFTER YOUR THOUGHTS, STRAIGHT BACK AGAIN TO *FRANCE.*

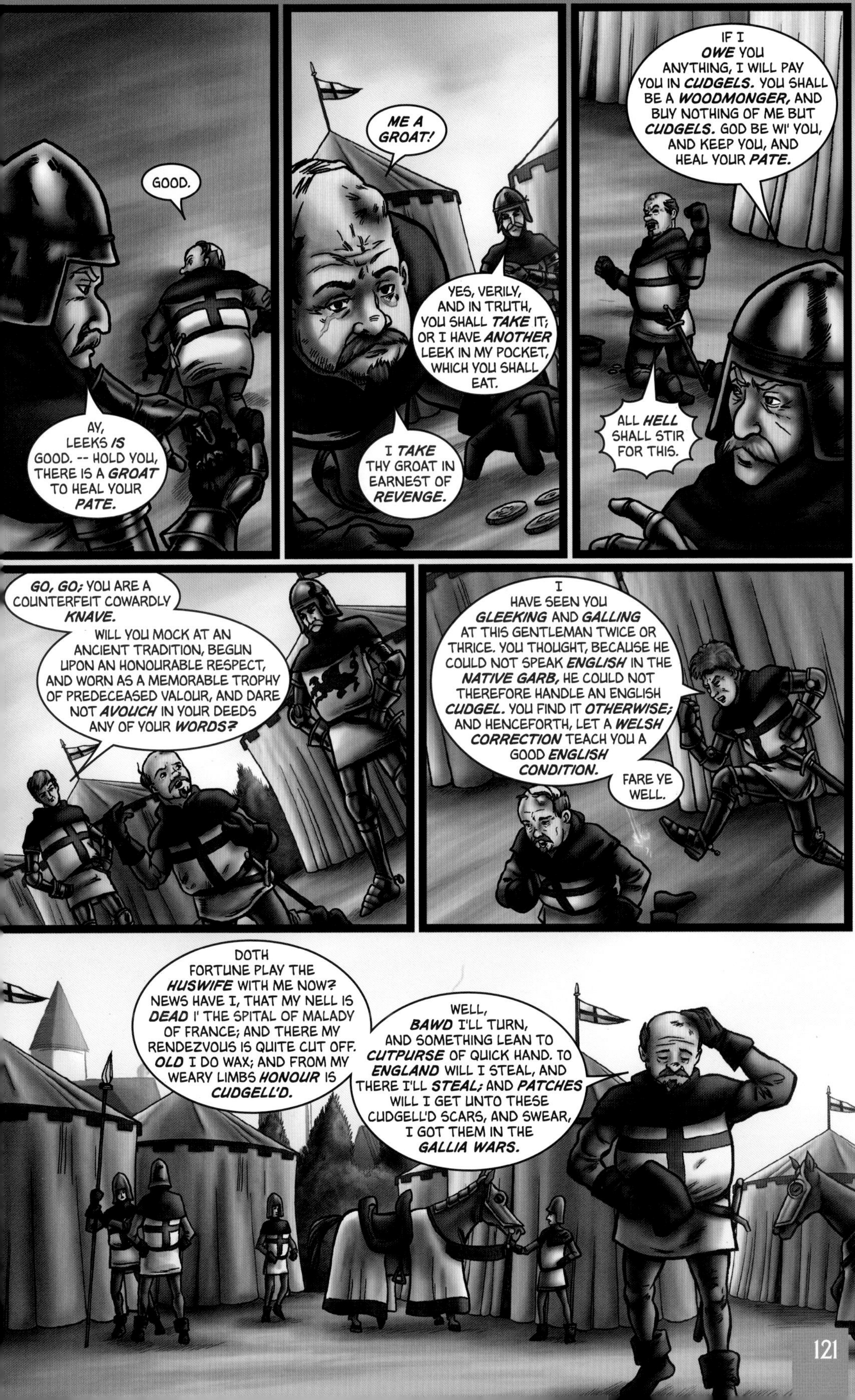
GOOD.
AY, LEEKS IS GOOD. -- HOLD YOU, THERE IS A GROAT TO HEAL YOUR PATE.
ME A GROAT!
YES, VERILY, AND IN TRUTH, YOU SHALL TAKE IT; OR I HAVE ANOTHER LEEK IN MY POCKET, WHICH YOU SHALL EAT.
I TAKE THY GROAT IN EARNEST OF REVENGE.
IF I OWE YOU ANYTHING, I WILL PAY YOU IN CUDGELS. YOU SHALL BE A WOODMONGER, AND BUY NOTHING OF ME BUT CUDGELS. GOD BE WI' YOU, AND KEEP YOU, AND HEAL YOUR PATE.
ALL HELL SHALL STIR FOR THIS.
GO, GO; YOU ARE A COUNTERFEIT COWARDLY KNAVE.
WILL YOU MOCK AT AN ANCIENT TRADITION, BEGUN UPON AN HONOURABLE RESPECT, AND WORN AS A MEMORABLE TROPHY OF PREDECEASED VALOUR, AND DARE NOT AVOUCH IN YOUR DEEDS ANY OF YOUR WORDS?
I HAVE SEEN YOU GLEEKING AND GALLING AT THIS GENTLEMAN TWICE OR THRICE. YOU THOUGHT, BECAUSE HE COULD NOT SPEAK ENGLISH IN THE NATIVE GARB, HE COULD NOT THEREFORE HANDLE AN ENGLISH CUDGEL. YOU FIND IT OTHERWISE; AND HENCEFORTH, LET A WELSH CORRECTION TEACH YOU A GOOD ENGLISH CONDITION.
FARE YE WELL.
DOTH FORTUNE PLAY THE HUSWIFE WITH ME NOW? NEWS HAVE I, THAT MY NELL IS DEAD I' THE SPITAL OF MALADY OF FRANCE; AND THERE MY RENDEZVOUS IS QUITE CUT OFF. OLD I DO WAX; AND FROM MY WEARY LIMBS HONOUR IS CUDGELL'D.
WELL, BAWD I'LL TURN, AND SOMETHING LEAN TO CUTPURSE OF QUICK HAND. TO ENGLAND WILL I STEAL, AND THERE I'LL STEAL; AND PATCHES WILL I GET UNTO THESE CUDGELL'D SCARS, AND SWEAR, I GOT THEM IN THE GALLIA WARS.

TO CRY *AMEN* TO THAT, THUS WE APPEAR.

MY *DUTY* TO YOU BOTH, ON EQUAL LOVE, GREAT KINGS OF FRANCE AND ENGLAND, THAT I HAVE LABOUR'D, WITH ALL MY *WITS*, MY *PAINS*, AND *STRONG ENDEAVOURS*, TO BRING YOUR MOST IMPERIAL MAJESTIES UNTO THIS BAR AND ROYAL INTERVIEW, YOUR MIGHTINESS ON BOTH PARTS BEST CAN WITNESS.

SINCE THEN MY OFFICE HATH SO FAR PREVAIL'D THAT, *FACE TO FACE* AND ROYAL *EYE TO EYE*, YOU HAVE CONGREETED, LET IT NOT DISGRACE ME IF I DEMAND, BEFORE THIS ROYAL VIEW, WHAT *RUB* OR WHAT *IMPEDIMENT* THERE IS, WHY THAT THE NAKED, POOR, AND MANGLED *PEACE*, DEAR NURSE OF ARTS, PLENTIES, AND JOYFUL BIRTHS, SHOULD NOT IN THIS BEST GARDEN OF THE WORLD, OUR FERTILE FRANCE, PUT UP HER *LOVELY VISAGE?*

YOU ENGLISH PRINCES ALL, I DO *SALUTE* YOU.

ALAS! SHE HATH FROM FRANCE TOO *LONG* BEEN CHAS'D, AND ALL HER HUSBANDRY DOTH LIE ON HEAPS, *CORRUPTING* IN ITS OWN FERTILITY. HER *VINE*, THE MERRY CHEERER OF THE HEART, *UNPRUNED* DIES;

HER HEDGES EVEN-PLEACH'D, LIKE PRISONERS WILDLY OVERGROWN WITH HAIR, PUT FORTH *DISORDER'D TWIGS;* HER FALLOW LEAS THE *DARNEL, HEMLOCK,* AND RANK *FUMITORY,* DOTH ROOT UPON, WHILE THAT THE COULTER *RUSTS* THAT SHOULD *DERACINATE* SUCH SAVAGERY;

THE EVEN MEAD, THAT ERST BROUGHT SWEETLY FORTH THE FRECKLED *COWSLIP, BURNET,* AND *GREEN CLOVER,* WANTING THE SCYTHE, ALL UNCORRECTED, RANK, CONCEIVES BY IDLENESS, AND NOTHING TEEMS BUT HATEFUL *DOCKS,* ROUGH *THISTLES, KECKSIES, BURS,* LOSING BOTH *BEAUTY* AND *UTILITY;*

AND AS OUR VINEYARDS, FALLOWS, MEADS, AND HEDGES, DEFECTIVE IN THEIR NATURES, GROW TO *WILDNESS.* EVEN SO OUR *HOUSES,* AND *OURSELVES,* AND *CHILDREN,* HAVE LOST, OR DO NOT LEARN FOR WANT OF TIME, THE *SCIENCES* THAT SHOULD *BECOME* OUR COUNTRY; BUT GROW LIKE *SAVAGES,* -- AS SOLDIERS WILL, THAT NOTHING DO BUT MEDITATE ON BLOOD, -- TO *SWEARING* AND *STERN LOOKS, DIFFUS'D ATTIRE,* AND EVERYTHING THAT SEEMS *UNNATURAL.*

WHICH TO REDUCE INTO OUR FORMER FAVOUR YOU ARE ASSEMBLED; AND MY SPEECH ENTREATS THAT I MAY KNOW THE *LET,* WHY GENTLE *PEACE* SHOULD NOT EXPEL THESE INCONVENIENCES, AND BLESS US WITH HER *FORMER* QUALITIES.

123

124

FAIR KATHERINE, AND MOST FAIR! WILL YOU VOUCHSAFE TO TEACH A *SOLDIER* TERMS SUCH AS WILL ENTER AT A LADY'S EAR AND PLEAD HIS *LOVE-SUIT* TO HER GENTLE HEART?

YOUR MAJESTY SHALL *MOCK* AT ME; I CANNOT SPEAK YOUR *ENGLAND.*

O FAIR KATHERINE! IF YOU WILL *LOVE* ME *SOUNDLY* WITH YOUR FRENCH HEART, I WILL BE GLAD TO HEAR YOU CONFESS IT *BROKENLY* WITH YOUR ENGLISH TONGUE. DO YOU *LIKE* ME, KATE?

PARDONNEZ-MOI, I CANNOT TELL VAT IS "*LIKE ME.*"

AN *ANGEL* IS LIKE YOU, KATE, AND YOU ARE LIKE AN ANGEL.

QUE DIT-IL? QUE JE SUIS SEMBLABLE À LES ANGES?

I *SAID* SO, DEAR KATHERINE, AND I MUST NOT *BLUSH* TO *AFFIRM* IT.

OUI, VRAIMENT, SAUF VOTRE GRÂCE, AINSI DIT-IL.

O BON DIEU! LES LANGUES DES HOMMES SONT PLEINES DE *TROMPERIES.*

WHAT *SAYS* SHE, FAIR ONE? THAT THE *TONGUES OF MEN* ARE FULL OF *DECEITS?*

OUI, DAT DE TONGUES OF DE MANS IS BE FULL OF DECEITS: *DAT* IS DE PRINCESS.

THE PRINCESS IS THE *BETTER ENGLISHWOMAN.* I' FAITH, KATE, MY *WOOING* IS FIT FOR THY UNDERSTANDING: I AM *GLAD* THOU CANST SPEAK NO BETTER ENGLISH; FOR IF THOU *COULDST,* THOU WOULDST FIND ME SUCH A *PLAIN* KING THAT THOU WOULDST THINK, I HAD SOLD MY *FARM* TO BUY MY CROWN.

I KNOW NO WAYS TO MINCE IT IN LOVE, BUT DIRECTLY TO SAY, "*I LOVE YOU*";

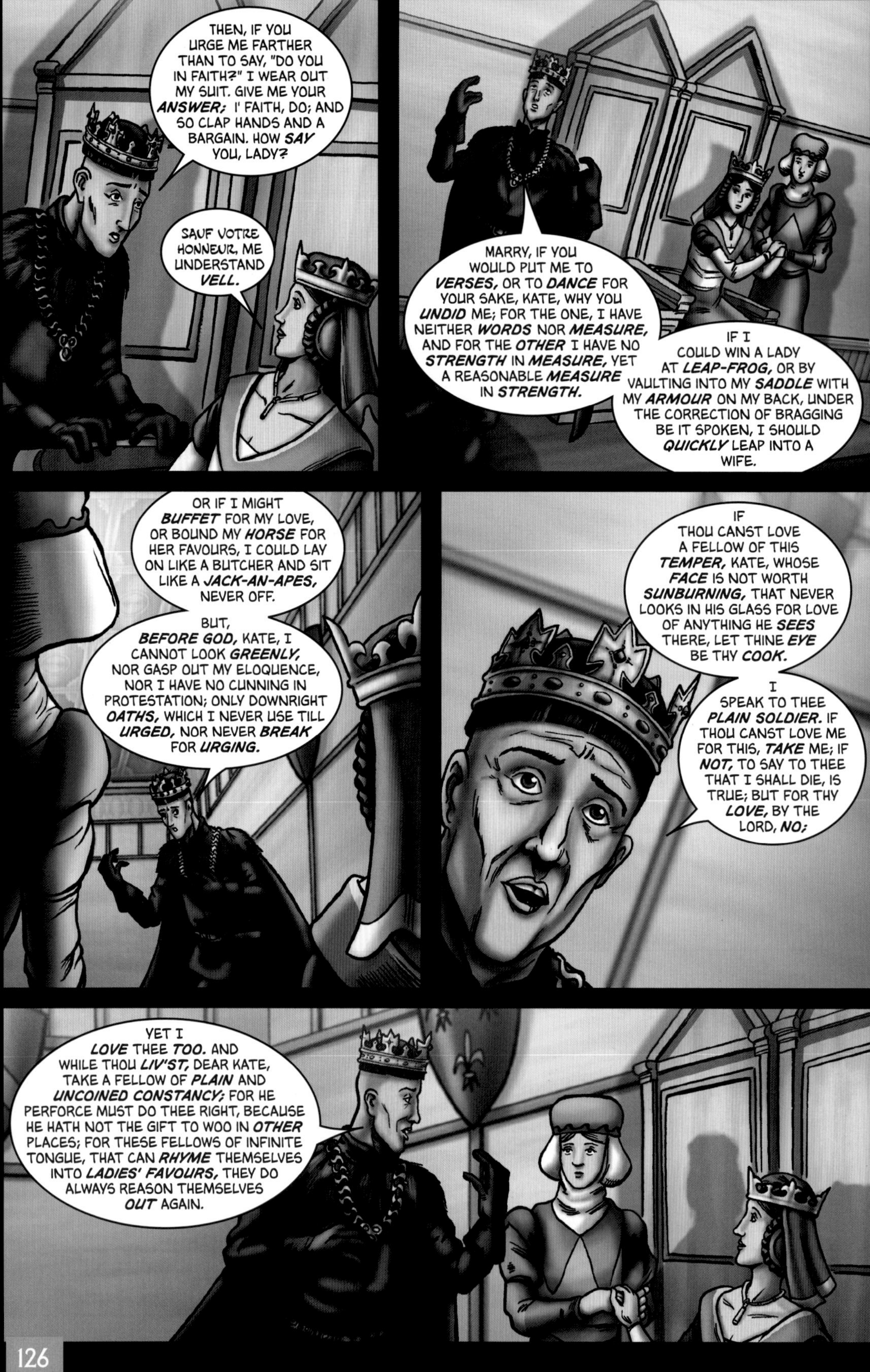

THEN, IF YOU URGE ME FARTHER THAN TO SAY, "DO YOU IN FAITH?" I WEAR OUT MY SUIT. GIVE ME YOUR ANSWER; I' FAITH, DO; AND SO CLAP HANDS AND A BARGAIN. HOW SAY YOU, LADY?
SAUF VOTRE HONNEUR, ME UNDERSTAND VELL.
MARRY, IF YOU WOULD PUT ME TO VERSES, OR TO DANCE FOR YOUR SAKE, KATE, WHY YOU UNDID ME; FOR THE ONE, I HAVE NEITHER WORDS NOR MEASURE, AND FOR THE OTHER I HAVE NO STRENGTH IN MEASURE, YET A REASONABLE MEASURE IN STRENGTH.
IF I COULD WIN A LADY AT LEAP-FROG, OR BY VAULTING INTO MY SADDLE WITH MY ARMOUR ON MY BACK, UNDER THE CORRECTION OF BRAGGING BE IT SPOKEN, I SHOULD QUICKLY LEAP INTO A WIFE.
OR IF I MIGHT BUFFET FOR MY LOVE, OR BOUND MY HORSE FOR HER FAVOURS, I COULD LAY ON LIKE A BUTCHER AND SIT LIKE A JACK-AN-APES, NEVER OFF.
BUT, BEFORE GOD, KATE, I CANNOT LOOK GREENLY, NOR GASP OUT MY ELOQUENCE, NOR I HAVE NO CUNNING IN PROTESTATION; ONLY DOWNRIGHT OATHS, WHICH I NEVER USE TILL URGED, NOR NEVER BREAK FOR URGING.
IF THOU CANST LOVE A FELLOW OF THIS TEMPER, KATE, WHOSE FACE IS NOT WORTH SUNBURNING, THAT NEVER LOOKS IN HIS GLASS FOR LOVE OF ANYTHING HE SEES THERE, LET THINE EYE BE THY COOK.
I SPEAK TO THEE PLAIN SOLDIER. IF THOU CANST LOVE ME FOR THIS, TAKE ME; IF NOT, TO SAY TO THEE THAT I SHALL DIE, IS TRUE; BUT FOR THY LOVE, BY THE LORD, NO;
YET I LOVE THEE TOO. AND WHILE THOU LIV'ST, DEAR KATE, TAKE A FELLOW OF PLAIN AND UNCOINED CONSTANCY; FOR HE PERFORCE MUST DO THEE RIGHT, BECAUSE HE HATH NOT THE GIFT TO WOO IN OTHER PLACES; FOR THESE FELLOWS OF INFINITE TONGUE, THAT CAN RHYME THEMSELVES INTO LADIES' FAVOURS, THEY DO ALWAYS REASON THEMSELVES OUT AGAIN.

129

LAISSEZ, MON SEIGNEUR, LAISSEZ, LAISSEZ! MA FOI, JE NE VEUX POINT QUE VOUS ABAISSEZ VOTRE GRANDEUR EN BAISANT LA MAIN D'UNE DE VOTRE SEIGNEURIE INDIGNE SERVITEUR. EXCUSEZ-MOI, JE VOUS SUPPLIE, MON TRÈS-PUISSANT SEIGNEUR.

THEN I WILL KISS YOUR *LIPS*, KATE.

LES DAMES ET DEMOISELLES POUR ÊTRE BAISÉES DEVANT LEURS NOCES, IL N'EST PAS LA COUTUME DE FRANCE.

MADAME MY INTERPRETER, WHAT *SAYS* SHE?

DAT IT IS NOT BE DE *FASHION* POUR LES LADIES OF FRANCE, -- I CANNOT TELL VAT IS BAISER EN ANGLISH.

TO *KISS*.

YOUR MAJESTEE ENTENDRE BETTRE QU MOI.

IT IS NOT A FASHION FOR THE MAIDS IN FRANCE TO *KISS* BEFORE THEY ARE *MARRIED*, WOULD SHE SAY?

OUI, VRAIMENT.

O KATE, *NICE CUSTOMS* CURTSY TO *GREAT KINGS*. DEAR KATE, YOU AND I CANNOT BE CONFINED WITHIN THE WEAK LIST OF A COUNTRY'S *FASHION*.

WE ARE THE *MAKERS* OF MANNERS, KATE; AND THE LIBERTY THAT FOLLOWS OUR PLACES STOPS THE MOUTH OF ALL FIND-FAULTS, AS I WILL DO *YOURS*, FOR UPHOLDING THE NICE FASHION OF YOUR COUNTRY IN *DENYING* ME A *KISS*; THEREFORE, *PATIENTLY*, AND *YIELDING*.

YOU HAVE *WITCHCRAFT* IN YOUR LIPS, KATE; THERE IS MORE ELOQUENCE IN A SUGAR TOUCH OF THEM THAN IN THE TONGUES OF THE *FRENCH COUNCIL*;

AND *THEY* SHOULD SOONER PERSUADE HARRY O ENGLAND THAN A *GENERAL PETITIO OF MONARCHS.*

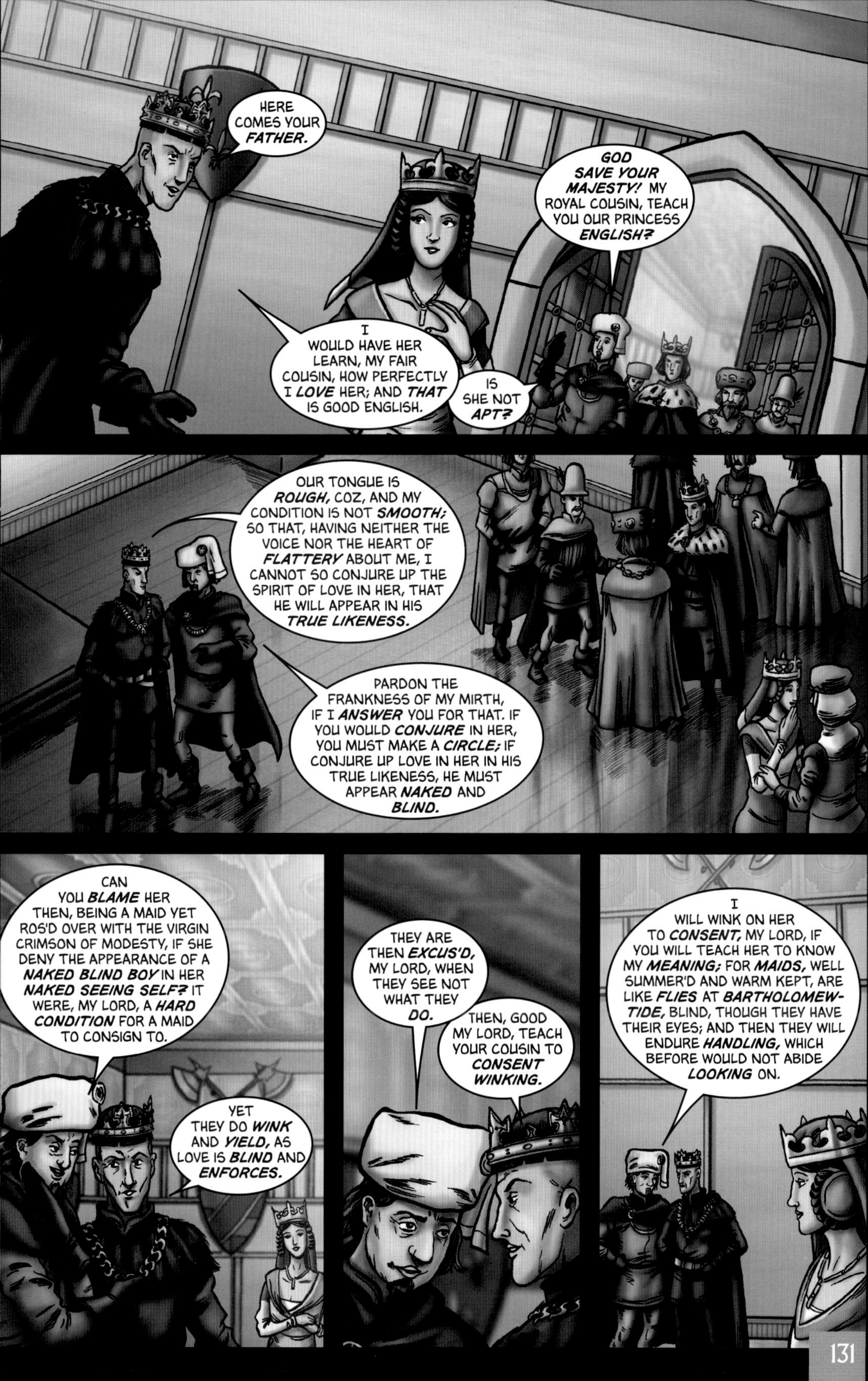
HERE COMES YOUR FATHER.
GOD SAVE YOUR MAJESTY! MY ROYAL COUSIN, TEACH YOU OUR PRINCESS ENGLISH?
I WOULD HAVE HER LEARN, MY FAIR COUSIN, HOW PERFECTLY I LOVE HER; AND THAT IS GOOD ENGLISH.
IS SHE NOT APT?
OUR TONGUE IS ROUGH, COZ, AND MY CONDITION IS NOT SMOOTH; SO THAT, HAVING NEITHER THE VOICE NOR THE HEART OF FLATTERY ABOUT ME, I CANNOT SO CONJURE UP THE SPIRIT OF LOVE IN HER, THAT HE WILL APPEAR IN HIS TRUE LIKENESS.
PARDON THE FRANKNESS OF MY MIRTH, IF I ANSWER YOU FOR THAT. IF YOU WOULD CONJURE IN HER, YOU MUST MAKE A CIRCLE; IF CONJURE UP LOVE IN HER IN HIS TRUE LIKENESS, HE MUST APPEAR NAKED AND BLIND.
CAN YOU BLAME HER THEN, BEING A MAID YET ROS'D OVER WITH THE VIRGIN CRIMSON OF MODESTY, IF SHE DENY THE APPEARANCE OF A NAKED BLIND BOY IN HER NAKED SEEING SELF? IT WERE, MY LORD, A HARD CONDITION FOR A MAID TO CONSIGN TO.
YET THEY DO WINK AND YIELD, AS LOVE IS BLIND AND ENFORCES.
THEY ARE THEN EXCUS'D, MY LORD, WHEN THEY SEE NOT WHAT THEY DO.
THEN, GOOD MY LORD, TEACH YOUR COUSIN TO CONSENT WINKING.
I WILL WINK ON HER TO CONSENT, MY LORD, IF YOU WILL TEACH HER TO KNOW MY MEANING; FOR MAIDS, WELL SUMMER'D AND WARM KEPT, ARE LIKE FLIES AT BARTHOLOMEW-TIDE, BLIND, THOUGH THEY HAVE THEIR EYES; AND THEN THEY WILL ENDURE HANDLING, WHICH BEFORE WOULD NOT ABIDE LOOKING ON.

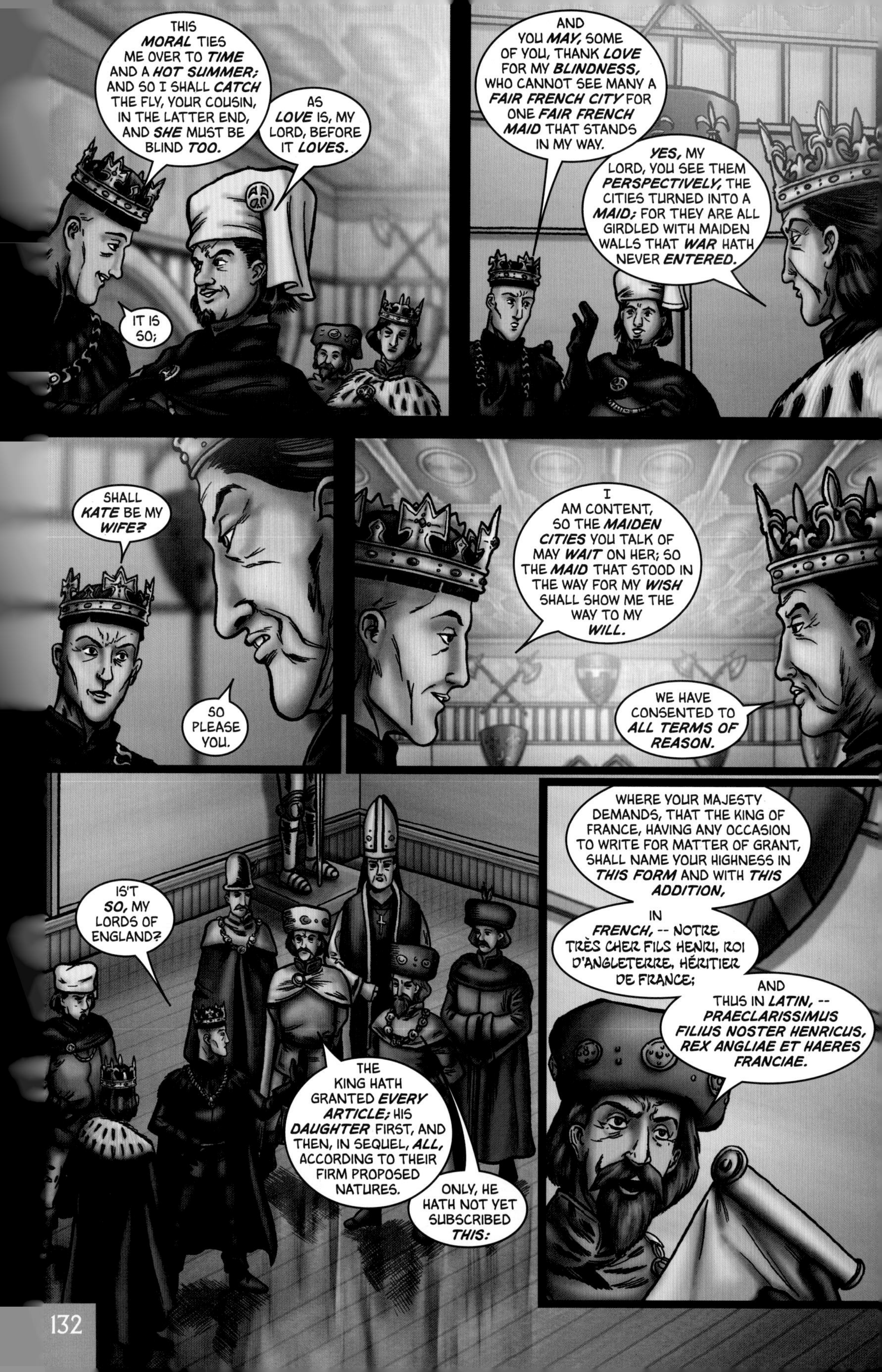
THIS MORAL TIES ME OVER TO TIME AND A HOT SUMMER; AND SO I SHALL CATCH THE FLY, YOUR COUSIN, IN THE LATTER END, AND SHE MUST BE BLIND TOO.
AS LOVE IS, MY LORD, BEFORE IT LOVES.
IT IS SO;
AND YOU MAY, SOME OF YOU, THANK LOVE FOR MY BLINDNESS, WHO CANNOT SEE MANY A FAIR FRENCH CITY FOR ONE FAIR FRENCH MAID THAT STANDS IN MY WAY.
YES, MY LORD, YOU SEE THEM PERSPECTIVELY, THE CITIES TURNED INTO A MAID; FOR THEY ARE ALL GIRDLED WITH MAIDEN WALLS THAT WAR HATH NEVER ENTERED.
SHALL KATE BE MY WIFE?
SO PLEASE YOU.
I AM CONTENT, SO THE MAIDEN CITIES YOU TALK OF MAY WAIT ON HER; SO THE MAID THAT STOOD IN THE WAY FOR MY WISH SHALL SHOW ME THE WAY TO MY WILL.
WE HAVE CONSENTED TO ALL TERMS OF REASON.
IS'T SO, MY LORDS OF ENGLAND?
THE KING HATH GRANTED EVERY ARTICLE; HIS DAUGHTER FIRST, AND THEN, IN SEQUEL, ALL, ACCORDING TO THEIR FIRM PROPOSED NATURES.
ONLY, HE HATH NOT YET SUBSCRIBED THIS:
WHERE YOUR MAJESTY DEMANDS, THAT THE KING OF FRANCE, HAVING ANY OCCASION TO WRITE FOR MATTER OF GRANT, SHALL NAME YOUR HIGHNESS IN THIS FORM AND WITH THIS ADDITION,
IN FRENCH, -- NOTRE TRÈS CHER FILS HENRI, ROI D'ANGLETERRE, HÉRITIER DE FRANCE;
AND THUS IN LATIN, -- PRAECLARISSIMUS FILIUS NOSTER HENRICUS, REX ANGLIAE ET HAERES FRANCIAE.

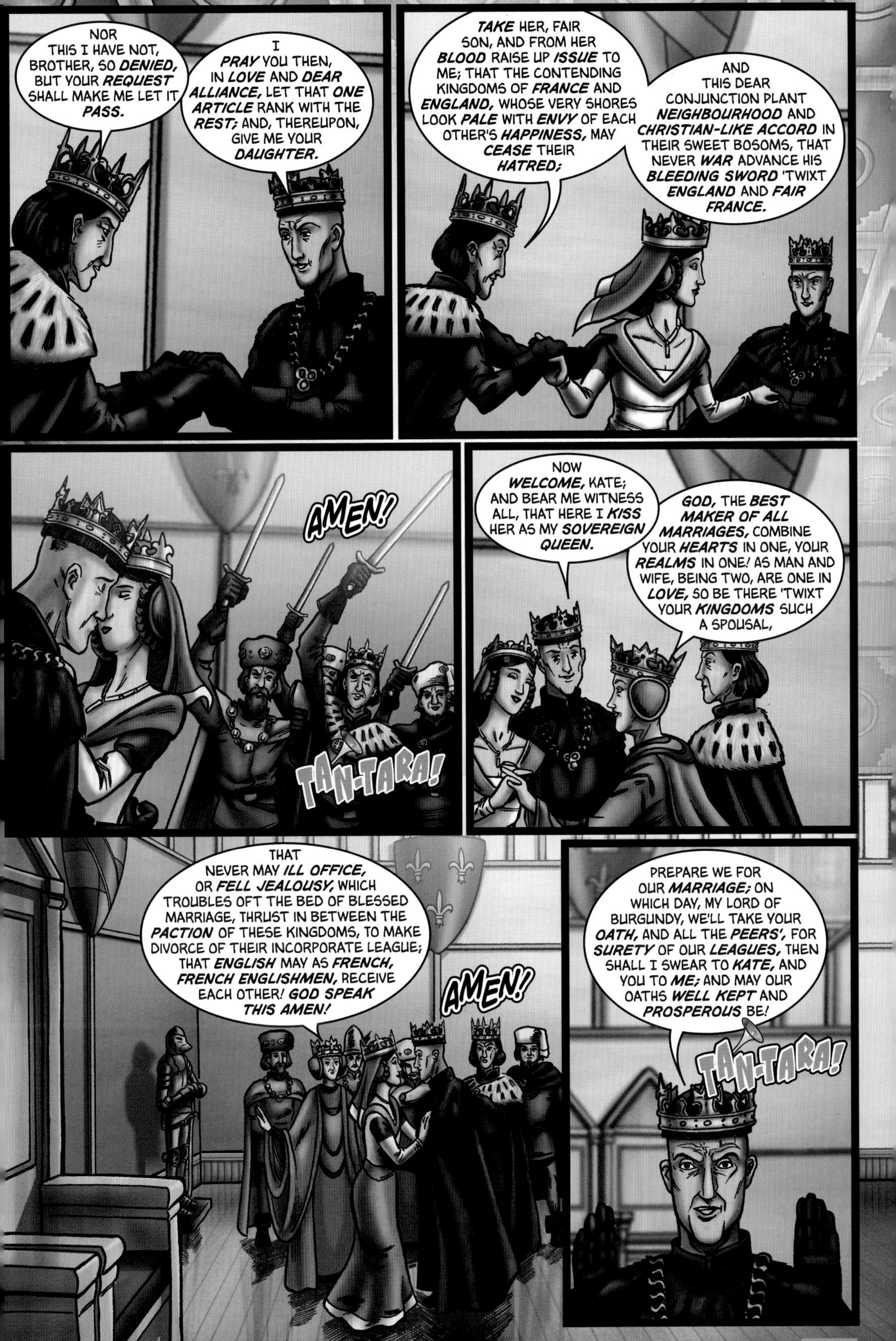
NOR THIS I HAVE NOT, BROTHER, SO DENIED, BUT YOUR REQUEST SHALL MAKE ME LET IT PASS.
I PRAY YOU THEN, IN LOVE AND DEAR ALLIANCE, LET THAT ONE ARTICLE RANK WITH THE REST; AND, THEREUPON, GIVE ME YOUR DAUGHTER.
TAKE HER, FAIR SON, AND FROM HER BLOOD RAISE UP ISSUE TO ME; THAT THE CONTENDING KINGDOMS OF FRANCE AND ENGLAND, WHOSE VERY SHORES LOOK PALE WITH ENVY OF EACH OTHER'S HAPPINESS, MAY CEASE THEIR HATRED;
AND THIS DEAR CONJUNCTION PLANT NEIGHBOURHOOD AND CHRISTIAN-LIKE ACCORD IN THEIR SWEET BOSOMS, THAT NEVER WAR ADVANCE HIS BLEEDING SWORD 'TWIXT ENGLAND AND FAIR FRANCE.
AMEN!
TAN-TARA!
NOW WELCOME, KATE; AND BEAR ME WITNESS ALL, THAT HERE I KISS HER AS MY SOVEREIGN QUEEN.
GOD, THE BEST MAKER OF ALL MARRIAGES, COMBINE YOUR HEARTS IN ONE, YOUR REALMS IN ONE! AS MAN AND WIFE, BEING TWO, ARE ONE IN LOVE, SO BE THERE 'TWIXT YOUR KINGDOMS SUCH A SPOUSAL,
THAT NEVER MAY ILL OFFICE, OR FELL JEALOUSY, WHICH TROUBLES OFT THE BED OF BLESSED MARRIAGE, THRUST IN BETWEEN THE PACTION OF THESE KINGDOMS, TO MAKE DIVORCE OF THEIR INCORPORATE LEAGUE; THAT ENGLISH MAY AS FRENCH, FRENCH ENGLISHMEN, RECEIVE EACH OTHER! GOD SPEAK THIS AMEN!
AMEN!
PREPARE WE FOR OUR MARRIAGE; ON WHICH DAY, MY LORD OF BURGUNDY, WE'LL TAKE YOUR OATH, AND ALL THE PEERS', FOR SURETY OF OUR LEAGUES, THEN SHALL I SWEAR TO KATE, AND YOU TO ME; AND MAY OUR OATHS WELL KEPT AND PROSPEROUS BE!
TAN-TARA!

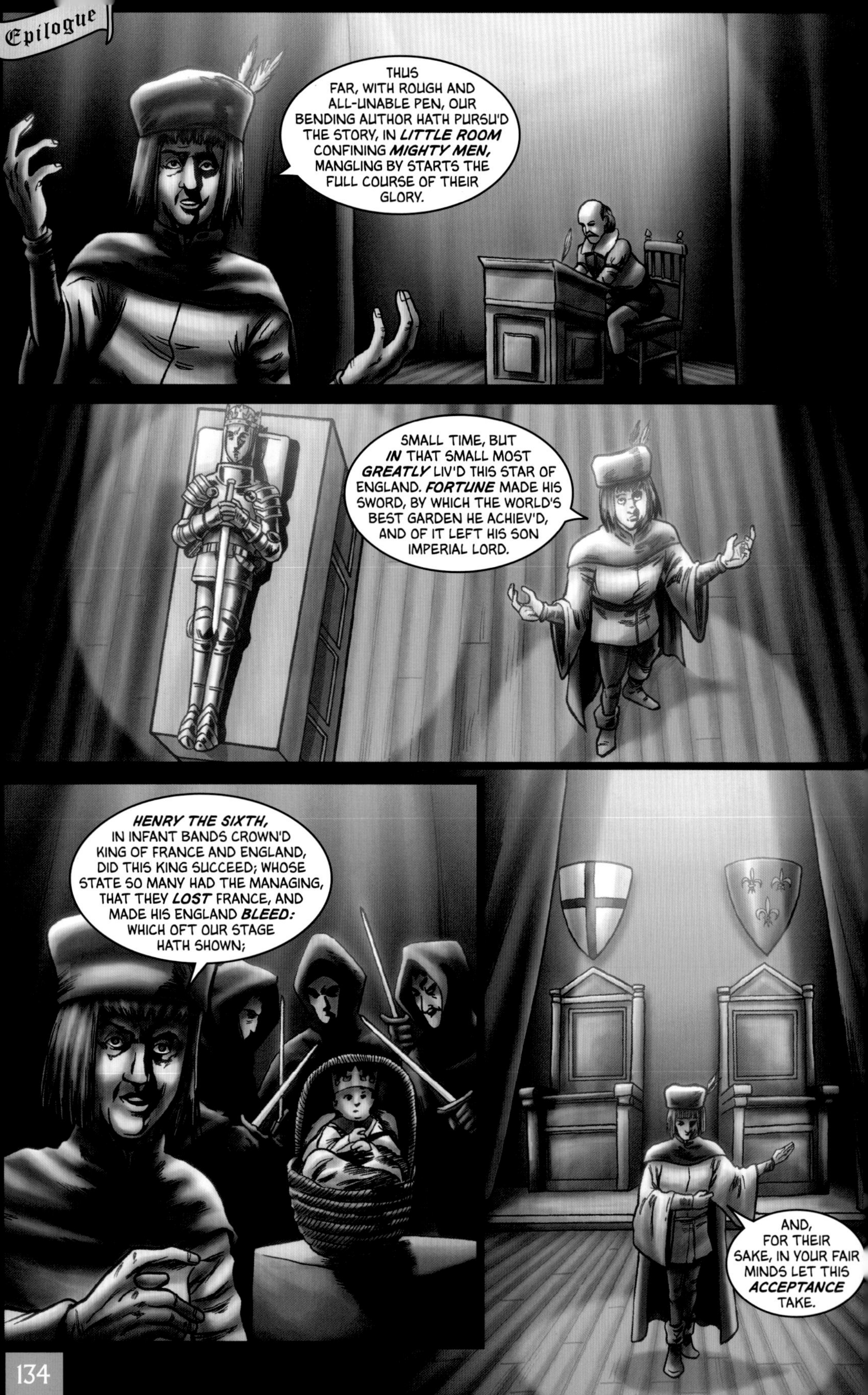
THUS FAR, WITH ROUGH AND ALL-UNABLE PEN, OUR BENDING AUTHOR HATH PURSU'D THE STORY, IN *LITTLE ROOM* CONFINING *MIGHTY MEN,* MANGLING BY STARTS THE FULL COURSE OF THEIR GLORY.
SMALL TIME, BUT *IN* THAT SMALL MOST *GREATLY* LIV'D THIS STAR OF ENGLAND. *FORTUNE* MADE HIS SWORD, BY WHICH THE WORLD'S BEST GARDEN HE ACHIEV'D, AND OF IT LEFT HIS SON IMPERIAL LORD.
HENRY THE SIXTH, IN INFANT BANDS CROWN'D KING OF FRANCE AND ENGLAND, DID THIS KING SUCCEED; WHOSE STATE SO MANY HAD THE MANAGING, THAT THEY *LOST* FRANCE, AND MADE HIS ENGLAND *BLEED:* WHICH OFT OUR STAGE HATH SHOWN;
AND, FOR THEIR SAKE, IN YOUR FAIR MINDS LET THIS *ACCEPTANCE* TAKE.

Henry V

End

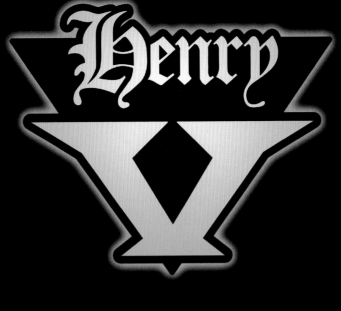

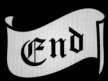

William Shakespeare

(c.1564 - 1616 AD)

National Portrait Gallery, London

William Shakespeare is one of the most widely read authors and possibly the best dramatist ever to live. The actual date of his birth is not known, but April 23rd 1564 (St George's Day) has traditionally been his accepted birthday, as this was three days before his baptism. He died on the same date in 1616, at the age of fifty-two.

The life of William Shakespeare can be divided into three acts. The first twenty years of his life were spent in Stratford-upon-Avon, where he grew up, went to school, got married and became a father. The next twenty-five years he spent as an actor and playwright in London. He spent his last few years back in Stratford-upon-Avon, where he enjoyed his retirement in moderate wealth gained from his successful years in the theater.

William, the third of eight children, was the eldest son of tradesman John Shakespeare and Mary Arden. His father was later elected mayor of Stratford, which was the highest post a man in civic politics could attain. In sixteenth-century England, William was lucky to survive into adulthood: syphilis, scurvy, smallpox, tuberculosis, typhus and dysentery shortened life expectancy at the time to approximately thirty-five years. The Bubonic Plague took the lives of many and was believed to have been the cause of death for three of William's seven siblings.

Little is known of William's childhood, but he is thought to have attended the local grammar school, where he studied Latin and English Literature. In 1582, at the age of eighteen, William married a local farmer's daughter, Anne Hathaway, who was eight years his senior and three months pregnant. During their marriage they had three children: Susanna, born on May 26th 1583, and twins, Hamnet and Judith, born on February 2nd 1585. Hamnet, William's only son, caught Bubonic Plague and died at the age of eleven.

Five years into his marriage, William moved to London and appeared in many small parts at The Globe Theatre, then one of the biggest theaters in England. His first appearance in public as a poet was in 1593 with *Venus and Adonis* and again in the following year with *The Rape of Lucrece*. Six years later, in 1599, he became joint proprietor of The Globe Theatre.

When Queen Elizabeth died in 1603, she was succeeded by her cousin King James of Scotland. King James supported Shakespeare and his band of actors and gave them license to call themselves "The King's Men" in return for entertaining the court.

In just twenty-three years, between 1590 and 1613, William Shakespeare is attributed with writing thirty-eight plays, one-hundred-and-fifty-four sonnets and five poems. No original manuscript exists for any of his plays, so it is hard to date them accurately. However, from their contents and reports at the time, it is believed that his first play was ***The Taming of the Shrew*** and that his last complete work was ***Two Noble Kinsmen***, written two years before he died. The cause of his death remains unknown.

He was buried on April 25th 1616, two days after his death, at the Church of the Holy Trinity (the same Church where he had been baptized fifty-two years earlier). His gravestone bears these words, believed to have been written by William himself:-

"Good friend for Jesus sake forbear,
To dig the dust enclosed here!
Blest be the man that spares these stones,
And curst be he that moves my bones"

At the time of his death, William had substantial properties, which he bestowed on his family and associates from the theater.

In his will he left his wife, the former Anne Hathaway, his second best bed!

William Shakespeare's last direct descendant died in 1670. She was his granddaughter, Elizabeth.

Henry V, King of England

(c.1387 - 1422 AD)

One of the great warrior kings of medieval England, Henry is most famous for his victory against the French at the Battle of Agincourt.

Henry V, the eldest son of Henry IV and Mary Bohun, was born in 1387. He became Prince of Wales at his father's coronation in 1399. Henry was an accomplished soldier: at fourteen he fought the Welsh forces of Owain Glyndwr; in 1403, aged sixteen, he commanded his father's forces at the battle of Shrewsbury. He was also keen to have a role in government, leading to many disagreements with his father. Henry became king in 1413.

In 1415, he successfully crushed an uprising designed to put Edmund Mortimer, Earl of March, on the throne. Shortly afterwards he sailed for France, which was to be the focus of his attentions for most of his reign. Henry was determined to regain the lands in France previously held by his ancestors and so laid his claim to the French throne. The French war served two purposes - to gain lands lost in previous battles and to focus attention away from any of his cousins' royal ambitions.

He first captured the port of Harfleur and then on October 25th 1415 defeated the French at the Battle of Agincourt. Between 1417 and 1419 Henry followed up this success with the conquest of Normandy. Rouen surrendered in January 1419 and his successes forced the French to agree to the Treaty of Troyes in May 1420.

Henry was recognized as heir to the French throne and married Katherine, the daughter of the French king. In February 1421, Henry returned to England for the first time in three-and-a-half years, and he and Katherine undertook a royal progress around the country. In June, he returned to France and died suddenly, probably of dysentery, on August 31st 1422. His nine-month-old son succeeded him as King of England (Henry never

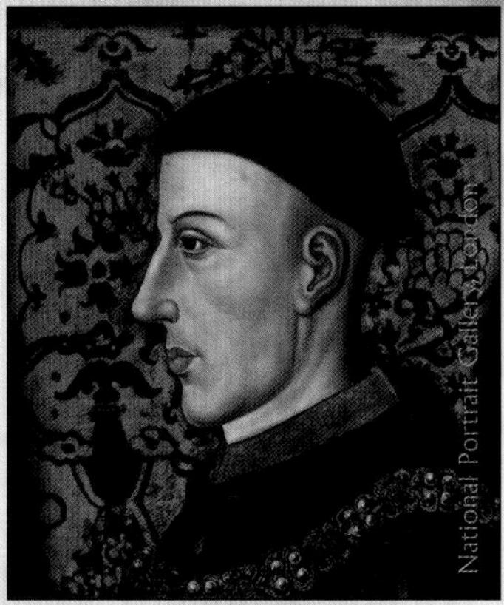
National Portrait Gallery, London

saw his child). Had Henry lived a mere two months longer, he would have been king of both England and France.

The Elizabethan historian Rafael Holinshed, in his ***Chronicles of England***, summed up Henry's reign as such: "This Henry was a king, of life without spot, a prince whom all men loved, and of none disdained, a captain against whom fortune never frowned, nor mischance once spurned, whose people him so severe a justicer both loved and obeyed (and so humane withal) that he left no offence unpunished, nor friendship unrewarded; a terror to rebels, and suppressor of sedition, his virtues notable, his qualities most praiseworthy."

The Battle of Agincourt October 25th, 1415 (St. Crispin's Day)

"From the thirteenth until the sixteenth century, the national weapon of the English army was the longbow. It was this weapon which conquered Wales and Scotland, gave the English their victories in the Hundred Years War, and permitted England to replace France as the foremost military power in Medieval Europe. The longbow was the machine gun of the Middle Ages: accurate, deadly, possessed of a long-range and rapid rate of fire, the flight of its missiles was liken to a storm. Cheap and simple enough for the yeoman to own and master, it made him superior to a knight on the field of battle."

The Medieval English Longbow
by Robert E. Kaiser, M.A.

Henry V, King of England, and (according to him and his advisors), parts of France, invaded France on August 13th, 1415 to claim by force his French Kingdom. He first laid siege to the port of Harfleur, in the classic medieval style using primitive cannons (bombards), trenches and ramparts encircling the town's walls. Harfleur finally fell on September 22nd and on October 8th Henry's by now smaller, starving and weary army of some 5,000 archers and 1,000 men-at-arms began a 260-mile march to Calais, hoping to reach England before winter set in.

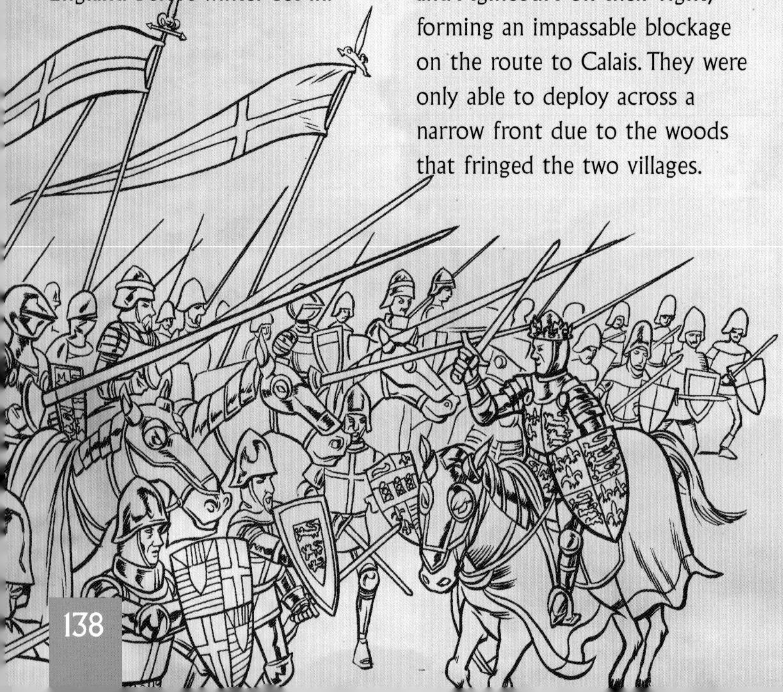

The main French army started from Rouen in pursuit of the English. On October 24th Henry's scouts spotted the French army near the little river of Ternoise, completely blocking the path to Calais. Henry now had no choice but to give battle to the far larger French army of some 15,000-36,000 men (as accurate an estimate as can be given!)

October 25th dawned cold and wet, with the French army drawn up between the villages of Tramecourt on their left flank and Agincourt on their right, forming an impassable blockage on the route to Calais. They were only able to deploy across a narrow front due to the woods that fringed the two villages.

The English army was gathered in between the woods at the other end of the field, roughly a mile from the French.

This meant that the battle took place on recently plowed fields between the woods - a decisive factor in the final outcome.

The French formed three massive divisions (called "battles"), with the first two consisting of dismounted men-at-arms with cavalry on their flanks, and a third division consisting entirely of cavalry. Crossbowmen and archers were to take up position at the front of the divisions.

The French planned to shower the English with arrows, then move in with the flanking cavalry to take out the bowmen of the English army, as the French men-at-arms moved in to dispatch the English infantry.

By 11am the English could wait no longer for a French advance. Henry's troops were tired and weak from hunger, dysentery and the long, wet march; so they advanced to within 250 yards of the French troops. At this point the English archers halted and pounded in pointed wooden stakes (palings) in front of their positions to keep the French cavalry at bay.

Charles d'Albret
Agincourt
Tramecourt
Archers
Archers
Camoys
Henry V
York

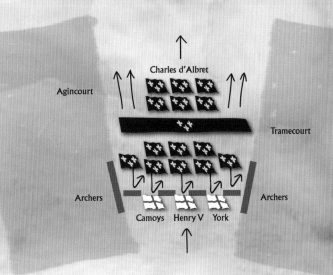

The English advance threw the French into confusion and forced the premature charge of the French heavy cavalry. The cavalry advanced slowly in the mud and under a hail of arrows. They tried to outflank the English but were hemmed in by the woods and forced to continue with a frontal assault. They quickly found themselves and their horses impaled upon the stakes and under unremitting fire from the English archers. The English line held and what was left of the French cavalry was forced to withdraw.

The first French division of men-at-arms lumbered forward after the failure of the cavalry assault. The English arrows took their toll but the French finally closed with the English men-at-arms. Many French nobles had already been killed by arrows and, as the line pushed forward, many more men fell and were trampled to death, hampered by their heavy armor.

Initially the impact of the French advance drove the English line back, but they quickly recovered; and the English men-at-arms and archers joined the fray with mallets, axes and swords, easily dispatching the tightly packed and heavily armored columns of French knights. As the first French division was being decimated, the remaining English archers kept up a heavy hail of arrows on the advancing second French division of men-at-arms. The knights in this second division saw what was happening to their comrades and began leaving the field without engaging the English. This left the mounted French third division as the last hope for the French to gain victory from defeat. However attacking the English longbowmen was more than those troops wished to contemplate and they too began drifting away through the Tramecourt Woods.

The English interpreted this movement as a potential threat, with the French moving through the woods and possibly threatening the English from the rear. This news, coupled with reports that the English baggage train had been attacked, led Henry to order the deaths of all the prisoners, as there were not enough soldiers left to guard the prisoners and fend off a further attack.

Many prisoners were killed but some English knights who were horrified by this order saved their prisoners. It is believed that more French deaths took place during this slaughter, than during the battle itself.

By the end of the day it is estimated that between 7,000 and 10,000 French had perished but only 500 English. Henry and his army went on to Calais and then back to England, with a number of French nobles held to ransom.

It was an incredible English victory that would go down in the annals of warfare.

Arguably, the deciding factor for the outcome was the terrain. The narrow field of battle, of recently plowed land hemmed in by dense woodland, favored the English.

However, Shakespeare appears to have exploited a rather different rationale, basing the victory on the will of God, given that Henry's cause was just.

Page Creation

In order to create three versions of the same book, the play is first adapted into three scripts: Original Text, Plain Text and Quick Text. While the degree of complexity changes for each script, the artwork remains the same for all three books.

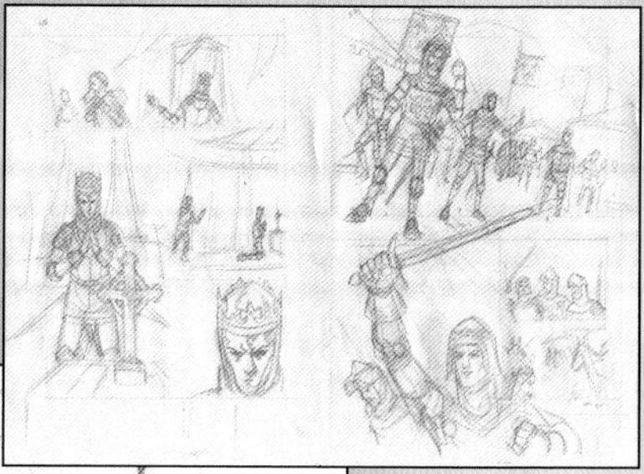

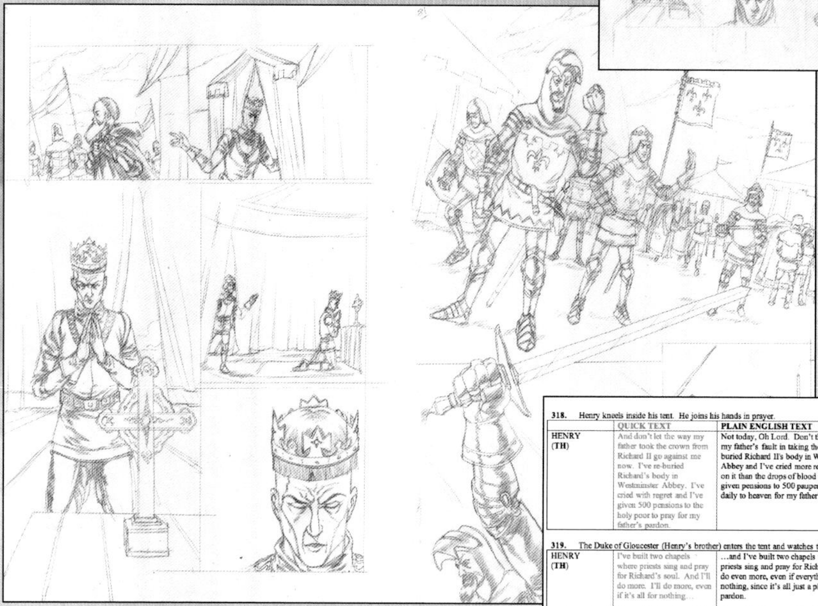

Above is a rough thumbnail sketch of pages 86 and 87 created from the script. Once the rough sketch is approved it is redrawn as a clean finished pencil sketch (left).

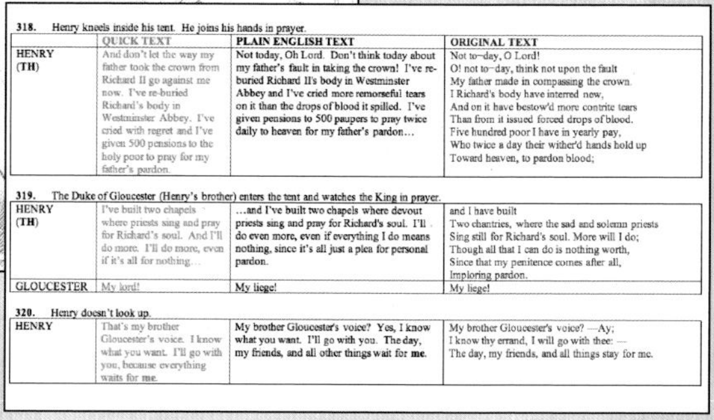

318. Henry kneels inside his tent. He joins his hands in prayer.

	QUICK TEXT	PLAIN ENGLISH TEXT	ORIGINAL TEXT
HENRY (TH)	And don't let the way my father took the crown from Richard II go against me now. I've re-buried Richard's body in Westminster Abbey. I've cried with regret and I've given 500 pensions to the holy poor to pray for my father's pardon.	Not today, Oh Lord. Don't think today about my father's fault in taking the crown! I've re-buried Richard II's body in Westminster Abbey and I've cried more remorseful tears on it than the drops of blood it spilled. I've given pensions to 500 paupers to pray twice daily to heaven for my father's pardon…	Not to–day, O Lord! O! not to–day, think not upon the fault My father made in compassing the crown. I Richard's body have interred new, And on it have bestow'd more contrite tears Than from it issued forced drops of blood. Five hundred poor I have in yearly pay, Who twice a day their wither'd hands hold up Toward heaven, to pardon blood;

319. The Duke of Gloucester (Henry's brother) enters the tent and watches the King in prayer.

HENRY (TH)	I've built two chapels where priests sing and pray for Richard's soul. And I'll do more. I'll do more, even if it's all for nothing…	…and I've built two chapels where devout priests sing and pray for Richard's soul. I'll do even more, even if everything I do means nothing, since it's all just a plea for personal pardon.	and I have built Two chantries, where the sad and solemn priests Sing still for Richard's soul. More will I do; Though all that I can do is nothing worth, Since that my penitence comes after all, Imploring pardon.
GLOUCESTER	My lord!	My liege!	My liege!

320. Henry doesn't look up.

HENRY	That's my brother Gloucester's voice. I know what you want. I'll go with you, because everything waits for me.	My brother Gloucester's voice? Yes, I know what you want. I'll go with you. The day, my friends, and all other things wait for me.	My brother Gloucester's voice? —Ay; I know thy errand, I will go with thee: — The day, my friends, and all things stay for me.

From the pencil sketch we can now create an inked version of the same page (below).

Inking is not simply tracing over the pencil sketch, it is the process of using black ink to fill in the shaded areas and to add clarity and cohesion to the "pencils".

The "inks" give us the final outline and the next stage is to add color to the inked image.

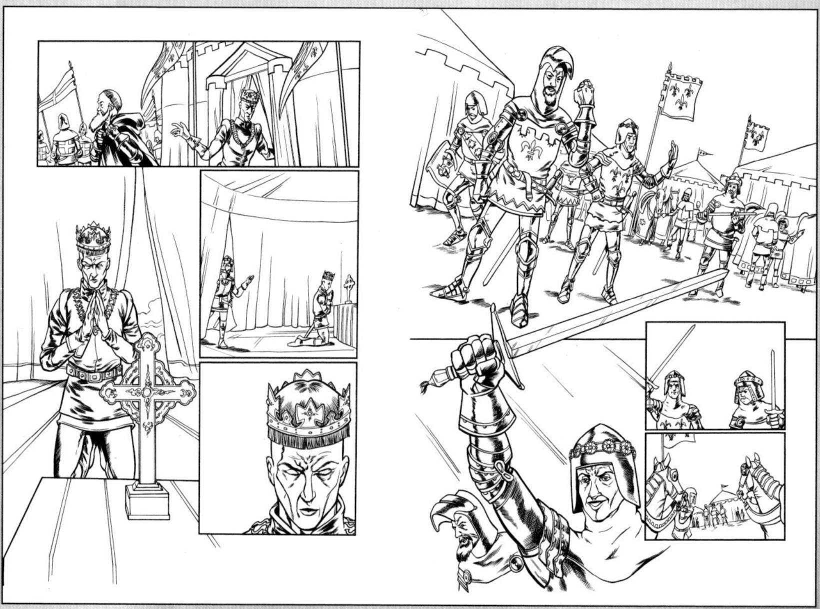

Adding color brings the page and its characters to life.

Each character has a detailed Character Study drawn. This is useful for the inkers and the colorists to refer to and ensures continuity throughout the book.

The last stage of page creation is to add the speech and any sound effects.

Speech bubbles are created from the script and are laid over the finished colored pages.

Three versions of lettered pages are produced for the three different versions of *Henry V*. These are then saved as final artwork pages and compiled into books.

Original Text

Plain Text

Quick Text

141

Shakespeare Around the Globe

The Globe Theatre and Shakespeare

It is hard to appreciate today how theaters were actually a new idea in William Shakespeare's time. The very first theater in Elizabethan London to show only plays, aptly called "The Theatre", was introduced by an entrepreneur by the name of James Burbage. In fact, "The Globe Theatre", possibly the most famous theater of that era, was built from the timbers of "The Theatre". The landlord of "The Theatre" was Giles Allen, a Puritan who disapproved of theatrical entertainment. When he decided to enforce a huge rent increase in the winter of 1598, the theater members dismantled the building piece by piece and shipped it across the Thames to Southwark for reassembly. Allen was powerless to do anything, as the company owned the wood - although he spent three years in court trying to sue the perpetrators!

The report of the dismantling party (written by Schoenbaum) says: **"ryotous... armed... with divers and manye unlawfull and offensive weapons... in verye ryotous outragious and forcyble manner and contrarye to the lawes of your highnes Realme... and there pulling breaking and throwing downe the sayd Theater in verye outragious violent and riotous sort to the great disturbance and terrefyeing not onlye of your subjectes... but of divers others of your majesties loving subjectes there neere inhabitinge."**

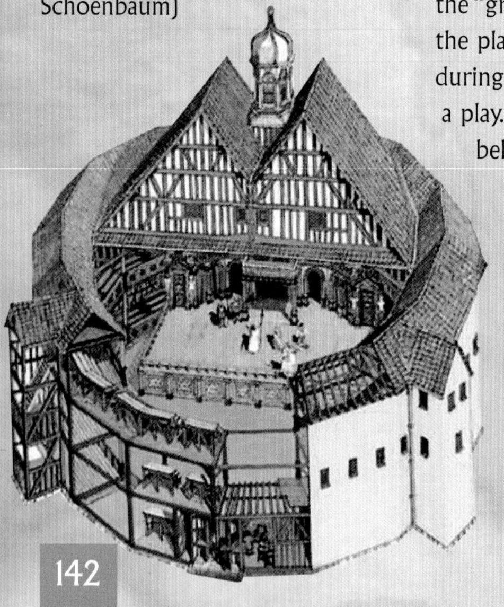

William Shakespeare became a part owner of this new Globe Theatre in 1599. It was one of four major theaters in the area, along with the Swan, the Rose, and the Hope. The exact physical structure of the Globe is unknown, although scholars are fairly sure of some details through drawings from the period. The theater itself was a closed structure with an open courtyard where the stage stood. Tiered galleries around the open area accommodated the wealthier patrons who could afford seats, and those of the lower classes - the "groundlings" - stood around the platform or "thrust" stage during the performance of a play. The space under and behind the stage was used for special effects, storage and costume changes. Surprisingly, although the entire structure was not very big by modern standards, it is known to have accommodated fairly large crowds - as many as 3,000 people - during a single performance.

The Globe II

In 1613, the original Globe Theatre burned to the ground when a cannon shot during a performance of ***Henry VIII*** set fire to the thatched roof of the gallery. Undeterred, the company completed a new Globe (this time with a tiled roof) on the foundations of its predecessor. Shakespeare didn't write any new plays for this theater. He retired to Stratford-Upon-Avon that year, and died two years later. Performances continued until 1642, when the Puritans closed down all theaters and places of entertainment. Two years later, the Puritans razed the building to the ground in order to build tenements upon the site. No more was to be seen of the Globe for 352 years.

Shakespeare's Globe

Led by the vision of the late Sam Wanamaker, work began on the construction of a new Globe in 1993, close to the site of the original theater. It was completed three years later, and Queen Elizabeth II officially opened the New Globe Theatre on June 12th 1997 with a production of ***Henry V.***

The New Globe Theatre is as faithful a reproduction as possible to the Elizabethan theater, given that the details of the original are only known from sketches of the time. The building can accommodate 1,500 people between the galleries and the "groundlings".

www.shakespeares-globe.org

There are also replica Globe theaters in Rome and Berlin and The Old Globe in San Diego. In New York, ambitious plans are underway to convert a decaying military fortification, built to defend America against the British in the War of 1812, into a New Globe – and amazingly, the existing structure has an identical footprint to Shakespeare's Globe Theatre in London.

New Globe Theater, New York

Shakespeare Today

Our fascination with William Shakespeare has not diminished over the centuries. Despite being written over 400 years ago, his plays are still read in schools, adapted into graphic novels(!), made into films, performed in theaters the world over, and are still taken to the public by acting troupes, such as **the British Shakespeare Company**. The tradition of open-air theater is deeply rooted in British culture. For over a thousand years companies have created theaters in the center of towns, erecting a pageant wagon or scaffolding stage from which to perform great historical and classical drama for a mass audience. These open-air acting troupes, which weathered the theatrical shifts from medieval Mystery and Morality plays to the sophisticated characterization of Elizabethan drama, were the inspiration behind the British Shakespeare Company (BSC). The pageant wagons, and later inn-yards and amphitheaters outside London, were for centuries the only means by which Shakespeare and others could communicate with audiences beyond the capital. Today, more than 100,000 people watch BSC performances each year. With a full company of players and performances that feature original live music and songs, beautiful period costumes and the magic of a summer's evening, the BSC is fulfilling that primary aim of all performers throughout the years: to enchant and delight audiences of all classes and ages. www.britishshakespearecompany.com

The Lord Chamberlain's Men are another open-air performance troupe, with the interesting, but authentic twist that all the parts are played by men (as was the case in Shakespeare's day). www.tcm.co.uk

In America, New York has Shakespeare in the Park. Since 1962, The Public Theater has staged productions of Shakespeare at The Delacorte Theater in Central Park. These performances are seen by approximately 80,000 New Yorkers and visitors each summer. In fact, since its inception, any of today's most acclaimed actors have taken part, including Patrick Stewart, Morgan Freeman, Meryl Streep, Denzel Washington, Kevin Kline and Jeff Goldblum. www.publictheater.org

Since 1997, Shakespeare 4 Kidz have been successfully providing an education in Shakespeare to children and young people all over the UK, and across the globe. Their unique approach has proved a hit with kids and adults alike. Their musicals have brought The Bard's work to life for thousands of people, and their creative education package is used extensively by teachers and education authorities throughout the UK. www.shakespeare4kidz.com

It seems that whatever time brings to our global society, and whatever developments take place within our cultures, William Shakespeare continues to have a place in our hearts and in our lives.

A UK publisher creating graphic novel adaptations of literary classics.
True to the original vision of the authors, our books have been further enhanced by using only the finest artists - giving you a truly wonderful reading experience that you'll return to again and again.

COMICS

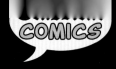

Henry V is available in three text formats, all using the same high quality artwork:

Henry
V
THE GRAPHIC NOVEL

Original Text
WE DOUBT NOT OF A FAIR AND LUCKY WAR, SINCE GOD SO GRACIOUSLY HATH BROUGHT TO LIGHT THIS DANGEROUS TREASON LURKING IN OUR WAY TO HINDER OUR BEGINNINGS: WE DOUBT NOT NOW BUT EVERY RUB IS SMOOTHED ON OUR WAY.
THEN FORTH, DEAR COUNTRYMEN! LET US DELIVER OUR PUISSANCE INTO THE HAND OF GOD, PUTTING IT STRAIGHT IN EXPEDITION. CHEERLY TO SEA! THE SIGNS OF WAR ADVANCE!
NO KING OF ENGLAND, IF NOT KING OF FRANCE!

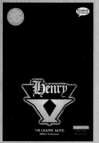

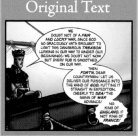

Original Text

This is the full, original script - just as The Bard intended. This version is ideal for purists, students and for readers who want to experience the unaltered text; but unlike a cold script, our beautiful artwork turns reading the play into a much more fulfilling experience. All of the text, all of the excitement!

Henry
V
THE GRAPHIC NOVEL
Plain Text

Plain Text
THERE'S NO DOUBT NOW THAT ALL OBSTACLES HAVE BEEN REMOVED. SO, MY COUNTRYMEN, LET'S GO!
LET'S DELIVER OUR ARMY INTO THE HAND OF GOD AND BEGIN OUR EXPEDITION IMMEDIATELY. AWAY TO SEA, WITH OUR WARLIKE ADVANCE!
I WON'T BE KING OF ENGLAND, IF I'M NOT ALSO KING OF FRANCE!

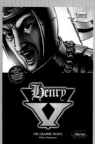

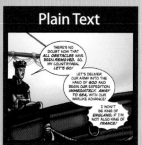

Plain Text

We take the original script and "convert" it into modern English, verse-for-verse. If you've ever wanted to fully appreciate the works of Shakespeare, but find the original language rather cryptic, then this is the version for you! This adaptation is ideal to help you fully understand the original text.

Henry
V
THE GRAPHIC NOVEL

Quick Text
THERE'S NOTHING ELSE IN OUR WAY, SO LET'S ADVANCE.
I WON'T BE KING OF ENGLAND, IF I'M NOT ALSO KING OF FRANCE!

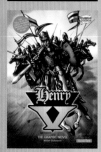

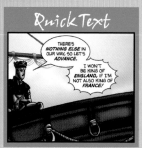

Quick Text

A revolution in graphic novels! We take the dialogue and reduce it to as few words as possible, but still retain the full essence of the story. This version allows readers to enter into and enjoy the stories quickly; and because the word balloons are smaller than in the other text versions, it also allows the fullest appreciation of our stunning artwork.

Classical Comics – Bringing Classics to Life!

OTHER CLASSICAL COMICS TITLES:

Macbeth

Macbeth

Published November 2008

A Christmas Carol

A Christmas Carol

Published November 2008

Jane Eyre

Jane Eyre

Published December 2008

Frankenstein

Frankenstein

Published December 2008

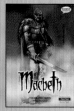

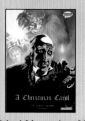

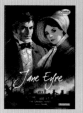

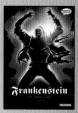